DEAD WRONG

CATH STAINCLIFFE

Constable & Robinson Ltd
55–56 Russell Square
London WC1B 4HP
www.constablerobinson.com

First published in the UK by Headline Book Publishing,
a division of Hodder Headline PLC, 1998

This paperback edition published in the UK by C&R Crime
an imprint of Constable & Robinson Ltd, 2013

A copy of the British Library Cataloguing in
Publication Data is available from the British Library.

ISBN: 978-1-47210-108-2 (paperback)

Typeset by TW Typesetting, Plymouth, Devon

Printed in the UK

1 3 5 7 9 10 8 6 4 2

For Mum and Dad – with love always

CHAPTER ONE

It never rains but it pours. Tell me about it. Everything had been quiet for weeks. So quiet I'd been reduced to serving injunctions and other papers for a solicitor – Rebecca Henderson of Platt, Henderson & Cockfoot. Yes, Cockfoot. Not exactly a drought of work but no more than a drizzle. Certainly not enough to top up the reservoirs of cash that I needed to keep myself and my daughter Maddie.

I hate delivering injunctions. It's a thankless task. The people you're finding don't want to be found. And they definitely don't want to receive the papers. I usually scarper as soon as they've got hold of the documents, before realization dawns, but some of them cotton on quick and are all for shooting the messenger.

I'm a fully paid-up coward when it comes to physical or even verbal aggression. Not only does it hurt like hell and do nasty things to your body, but it messes up your soul too. Scars on the inside as well as the outside. I've had my share of assaults and I'll do anything to reduce the risks of it happening again.

But despite my best intentions I've never been able to stick with regular self-defence classes. Life interrupts too often. My fallback position is to practise three simple moves whenever I remember – the knee to the balls, the fingers in the eyeballs, and the one to use when they've got you from behind: elbow in the ribs at the same time as you stamp hard on their feet. The follow-up to all of these is to run like mad.

Sometimes I take Digger, the house dog, with me for show. He's the sort of dog who would lie patiently waiting for me while I was being ripped limb from limb, but I bank on the fact that you can't tell that by looking. I have toyed with the idea of getting him one of those studded collars to beef up his image but I couldn't do it. I mean, I wouldn't be seen dead with a dog dressed like that. Undercover's all very well but I've got to draw the line somewhere.

The night that the monsoon began, so to speak, Digger and I were after Mr Kearsal in Belle Vue. There's not much of the old Belle Vue left, what with the East Manchester redevelopment. The dog track's still there – people are still going to the dogs in Manchester – but as far as housing goes there's just fragments left here and there, cut off from everything by the new wider roads and the barren industrial estates. Bleak places, shops and pubs long gone, they reek of neglect and isolation. Maybe they too are due for demolition, to be replaced by yet more superstores and petrol stations.

Number 53 was in the middle of the redbrick terrace. I parked a little way past it, checked I'd got the right envelope and reined in Digger. I left the car door open for a fast getaway.

The downstairs window was partly boarded up with wood on which someone had scrawled *Cantona and Giggs – the kings* in red. Someone else had scratched over this in black: *Giggs sucks – Man City rule*. Given that United had just won the Cup Final, while Manchester City had been relegated, this City fan's analysis displayed an incredible triumph of hope over reality (no bad thing for anyone having to live round there).

I knocked on the door. There was no answer. It was a muggy June evening, the sky a sullen blank holding onto its rain. I could hear the television from a neighbouring house and a child crying. I knocked again. Where was he? Evenings and early mornings were usually the best time to catch people in, though if they were unemployed they weren't best pleased to be woken up early by someone at the door. It was nearly seven; I'd timed it so if Mr Kearsal had any plans for going out that night, I'd be likely to get him before he left. I knocked again.

The door of the adjoining house opened and a woman stepped out. She'd short grey hair and glasses and wore a pinafore and mules straight out of the 1950s.

'Can I help, love?'

'I'm looking for Mr Kearsal,' I explained.

She shook her head. 'Not seen him about. Mind you, I don't – these days. Not since, let's think, last week sometime. You from the social work?'

'No.' I didn't want to tell her what I was doing there.

'Only they said they'd send someone, you see,' she pressed on, 'Victim Support or something, after the burglary. Shook him up, that did. I used to take him a bit of dinner now and then, if Harry and I were having a hot pot and that, or a nice bit of chicken – but he doesn't like to answer the door now. I mean, the stories you hear.'

I nodded, wondering where we were headed and whether to interrupt.

'Now he sometimes goes to his sister's in Ashton but he usually tells me, and he knows if he needs anything he can just bang on the wall – but he's not been himself since. It's aged him. You can see it. They took his wallet and then they duffed him up. Now what did they have to do that for?'

I murmured in sympathy.

'I could try calling for you if you like,' she offered. 'He might be in there but not wanting to open the door.'

'Thank you.'

'Who shall I say?'

'He doesn't know me.' I began to feel uncomfortable. If

this good neighbour knew I was serving debt-collection papers on him she wouldn't be so keen to help. 'I've some important papers for him.'

She nodded. She pushed the letter box back and put her mouth to the gap then stepped sharply back and turned away as if she'd been bitten.

'Are you all right?'

She shook her head emphatically, her eyes wild.

I shoved the papers in my pocket and dropped Digger's lead. I moved towards the door and pushed the metal flap up. The stench made me recoil as quickly as she had. As a child I'd once kept a bucketful of dead crabs in the shed, unknown to my parents. After a week they smelt like this.

I pulled my sweatshirt up to cover my nose and mouth and opening the flap again, peered in. I couldn't see anything but the dismal hallway. But when I turned my ear to the door and listened I heard the buzzing and humming of flies and, as I realized what they were doing there, my stomach finally rebelled and I turned to the road and threw up.

We rang the police from Mrs Grady's. I waited with her. I'd no desire to see what was left of Mr Kearsal, though I was curious about the manner of his death. It was hours before I could finally go, after countless cups of tea and Hobnobs.

The police arrived with vans and fancy tape and ambulances and men in suits. One of the suits came and talked to us, establishing who we were and our relationship to the deceased before noting the facts of our gruesome discovery. Mrs Grady was out in the kitchen busy making fresh tea when I was asked my name and the nature of my business in the area. I was glad she didn't have to learn that I was trying to serve papers on Mr Kearsal.

Outside, what neighbours there were had formed a little audience and Mrs Grady filled them in. The press arrived en masse from all the local free papers, plus the

Manchester Evening News, the local television and radio. I explained quickly to Mrs Grady that I didn't want to be interviewed or photographed. She looked at me as if I'd gone barmy but agreed and dutifully posed with another neighbour next to the police cordon.

One of the policemen made a brief statement to the effect that Mr Kearsal had been found hanging, and that at this stage there was no suspicion of foul play. A journalist asked if there'd been a note. Yes, a note had been recovered from the scene.

At long last I got Digger and myself into the car and home. I wondered on the way what the score was with Platt & Co. if I'd failed to serve the paper because the intended recipient was dead. Surely they'd pay me? Flipping heck, I deserved overtime and a bonus, given how long it had taken.

At home I had a shower to try and wash it all away. The sickly smell wouldn't go. I sprinkled lavender and rose oils round my room to try and disguise it, but I felt dirty still. I'd never known Mr Kearsal, never met him, but the fact that he had taken his own life was a chastening thought. And it was disturbing to think of him hanging there day after day, alone and unmourned.

I'd recently acquired a new answerphone which would let me ring it up and access my messages. This saved me having to traipse into the office just to check the machine. It's not that the office is far, it's only round the corner from the house, but some days I don't need to go in there at all. I called my new machine and it played me a message from Rebecca Henderson. She had a new job for me. How was I getting on with the last one?

I rang and got her, just as she was about to leave for court. I explained quickly about finding Mr Kearsal's corpse and mentioned how long I'd had to stay over in Belle Vue. I didn't have the gall to ask if I'd get paid – I was feeling guilty in an obscure sort of way. Perhaps if I hadn't tried to deliver the papers I wouldn't have stumbled on a suicide victim. If I'm not there it hasn't happened. Illogical yes, but sincerely felt.

Thankfully Rebecca is always direct; she comes out with what the rest of us are busy summoning up courage to mention. 'Sal, you poor thing, how awful. Look, we'll pay you for a day then. Send back the papers. Now, about this other matter . . .'

'Another injunction?'

'No, at least not at this stage. We've a new client who claims she's being followed. We want you to do some surveillance. Stalk the stalker, if you like. Establish dates and times, photos would be a help and we need to find out who he is.'

'She doesn't know him?' I was surprised. Most of the cases I'd heard about involved jilted lovers or ex-husbands.

'No, she's no idea. Can you do it?'

'Where does she live?'

'Chorlton. Works in town. He's turning up at both places.'

My mind flicked rapidly over all the implications, the major one being childcare arrangements.

'I can't do round the clock.'

'Shouldn't be necessary; we just need to establish what's actually going on, gather some evidence and see if we've enough to take out an injunction or press charges. Look, I must go. I've told her we'll be getting an investigator in so you might as well contact her directly and arrange to meet her.'

Rebecca gave me the name and number. I got through straight away. 'Debbie Gosforth? Hello, this is Sal Kilkenny here. I'm a private investigator. Rebecca Henderson asked me to get in touch with you.' I explained what Rebecca had told me, then asked when we could meet.

'Not now,' she said quickly, 'I've one of the children off ill. But I'm at work tomorrow – eleven till three. I could

6

meet you after that? Or Monday – I'm at home Mondays, but I'd rather it was tomorrow if you can.'

I hesitated, reluctant to use up the middle of a Saturday if I could avoid it. 'Could we do it before you start work?'

'Yeah, that should be all right.' She described a cafe near the Corn Exchange where we could meet. She sounded subdued over the phone; maybe she was tired from looking after the child she'd mentioned, or worn down by the experience of being followed by a stranger.

'How will I know who you are?' she asked.

'I'll wear a red jacket.'

'Not a pink carnation?'

I appreciated her attempt at humour (even if it wasn't exactly original) but her tone was too wistful to really pull it off.

There's no point in driving into town on a Saturday. Parking's difficult to find and outrageously expensive into the bargain. I got the bus into Piccadilly Gardens. It was a few minutes' walk down Market Street to the Corn Exchange.

Traffic was snarling up around the terminus and there seemed to be a lot of police vans around. As I reached the top of Market Street I ran into a crowd of people. I thought there'd been an accident, or maybe a robbery. The police helicopter flew overhead very low down. I turned to ask the man next to me if he knew what was going on.

Before he could answer, there was a great bang. Then nothing. A gust of air. I felt the surge in my stomach. A blast of wind and dust, strong enough to affect my balance. A cloud of smoke plumed into the sky. I thought I could hear screaming, lots of screaming. It was a chorus of alarms, shrilling and screeching.

They'd bombed the Arndale Centre.

CHAPTER TWO

Now if you'd asked me which building in Manchester I'd blow up, given the chance, the Arndale Centre would have come out tops (followed closely by the ghastly Piccadilly Plaza complex). Not just because of its ugly facade, like a giant toilet, all beige tiles and no windows, but also because of how the place made me feel when I was in there. It was horrible on the outside and terrifying on the inside. I always got lost and could never get out as quickly as I intended. It'd suck you in, just one more bargain, oh, just pop in there, in here, over there. When I finally made it to an exit I'd stagger out into the fresh air, reeling with exhaustion, blinking at natural light, appalled at how far I still was from the bus home. And how little of my list I'd actually bought. Best policy was to steer well clear of the place. Oh, I'd pop into the shops on the outside edge, off Market Street, but I'd be careful to come back out the same way and not get drawn into the back – the never-ending land of artificial lights, fancy tiled floors and piped music.

So it wasn't my favourite place. But this, this was terrible. My mouth was dry, I kept trying to swallow but I couldn't. My heart was racing and the rush of adrenalin had made my wrists prickle and the back of my neck burn.

This was real, this was savage. Standing there in the almost silent crowd, realization dawning. Murmurs, whispers. 'A bomb.'

Turning to each other, looking into each other's eyes and finding our own disbelief and horror mirrored there. There was clamour from the sirens and the alarms, the helicopter above, but we were quiet. Quiet and calm.

I stood for ages, bewildered. I was waiting for someone to tell me what to do. The police asked us to leave, to clear the area. It finally sank in that there was no way I'd be meeting up with Debbie Gosforth today. A clutch of German football supporters in lederhosen and multi-coloured knitted top hats asked me the way to their Princess Street hotel in subdued voices.

At long last I turned and began to walk home. It would be pointless waiting for a bus. As I made my way down Wilmslow Road people were stopping to exchange stories. Strangers in the city talking to each other with ease, united in crisis.

I'd no idea how many people might be dead, dying, hurt. Shocked rigid that this had happened here on a bright Saturday morning in a place always thronging with people.

The news hadn't reached my household. Ray Costello and his son Tom were in the garden, along with Maddie and Digger. I stood there, waiting for some reaction. Nothing. Ray finally clocked that I was behaving peculiarly.

'Sal?' he enquired, throwing the ball to Tom and walking my way.

'There's been a bomb,' I said, 'in town.'

He paled. 'Oh, God.'

I was so glad that there was someone at home to tell. It wasn't always easy living as we did, two single parents, each with a child, but I realized how much of a family the four of us were and how important that was to me. Ray and I don't have a relationship, not a sexual relationship, though people often assume we do. We started out as co-tenants, sharing the rent and the chores and taking turns to babysit, but over time we've become good friends and the arrangement has grown into something solid. We've built

9

a home together, somewhere we belong, safe and welcoming. A good place to raise our children.

The kids picked up the vibes immediately. Maddie looked over at me anxiously.

'I'm fine,' I reassured them. 'I'll put the kettle on.'

Ray followed me in. 'Whereabouts?'

'The Arndale, I think. It was all blocked off.' I put the radio on.

I couldn't stop shaking.

I listened to the local radio all afternoon, my eyes brimming with tears each time they read the headlines. It seemed as though no one had died though there were many people injured. Sunday was Father's Day and town had been full of children off to get something nice for Daddy. My mind kept turning to the people who'd have to live with the results of today for the rest of their lives. Had Debbie Gosforth been caught up in the blast? I'd leave it over the weekend, try ringing her on Monday.

Mid afternoon, our lodger Sheila rang; she was visiting friends in Blackburn for the weekend. Were we all right? What was going on? They'd heard about it on Radio 4 news. We exchanged words of shock. She would delay returning home, she told us; apparently there were no trains in or out of Victoria Station.

By the end of the day they were still talking about the injured rather than the dead. The first witnesses were on television; shoppers, medics.

The coverage rolled on all weekend. No one had been killed. It was a miracle. And in the teeth of all the chaos they went ahead with the football at Old Trafford – Germany versus Russia.

On Monday I rang my client.

'It's Sal Kilkenny, we were going to meet on Saturday. Are you all right?'

'Yes, I got stopped on the way in. It's a shock though.

Where I work, it's on Deansgate – it's in the cordon, you can't get in. I rang the boss to see what was happening. Even he can't go in yet. He's no idea if the shop's all right or when he'll open up again. It's awful. He doesn't know if the insurance will cover it. He doesn't even know if he can pay us.' She sighed.

'Can we rearrange our meeting?' I said. 'I can come to you at home or you can come here if you'd prefer.'

'You come to me,' she said.

'Today? This morning?'

'Yeah, I'm not going anywhere,' she said bitterly. The edge in her voice was a change from the resigned depression I'd heard during our last conversation.

I promised to be there in an hour's time. I walked the three hundred yards round the corner to my office first. I rent a cellar there in the Dobson family home. Grant and Jackie are teachers and during term time I hardly see them. Their four daughters are all at school or sixth form college. The arrangement works well. I can keep my work separate from my home, I can interview clients and store my papers there. The Dobsons seem to enjoy the curiosity value of a private eye in the basement. Not as noisy as a rock band, anyway.

I'd given the room a face-lift that spring: covered the old lilac paint on the walls and ceiling with a sandy yellow, lashed out on a big rag rug which covered most of the tatty carpet, painted the dining chairs and filing cabinet in bright citrus colours, pinned some filmy yellow muslin over the narrow basement window and stuck up a large, vivid blue silk-screen print that my friend Diane had done. The result was probably not what prospective clients expected from a private investigator's office, neither lawyerly nor seedy. But I loved it and it seemed to have a relaxing effect on people who were usually pretty tense and upset by the time they got to see me.

I prepared an invoice for Platt, Henderson & Cockfoot

for my valiant attempt to serve papers on the late Mr Kearsal, and got it ready to post. I collected my mail and checked my messages. Nothing important.

Debbie lived on Ivygreen Road, a street of terraced houses near busy Chorlton Green. Chorlton is a cosmopolitan district; the mix of housing means it caters for lots of different people. Not far from Manchester town centre and the universities, it has the added attraction of Chorlton Ees, a stretch of open meadows leading down to the River Mersey.

The long rows of identical red-brick terraces would easily look drab in the winter months, but in June the trees were in full leaf and people had placed hanging baskets here and there, and installed chimney pots and tubs in the tiny front gardens.

The Gosforth house was just like its neighbours, net curtains at the windows, neatly painted gate and door. Trim, unremarkable. The variety was in the choice of paint and the style of net. While some of them boasted frothing drapes and ruches like old-fashioned frilly baby pants, others went for sheer nets or the jardinière type with a convenient space in the centre of the windowsill to display a treasured ornament or plant. Debbie had chosen a bowl of dried flowers. The odd window without nets looked naked, shocking in its bravado, parading the life within to the world outside.

I rang the bell.

'Who is it?' Her caution in asking before opening the door was the first indication I had of how frightened this woman was.

'Sal Kilkenny.'

I heard her release the chain and then unlock the door.

Debbie invited me in and took me through to the living room, previously two rooms which had been knocked together to run the length of the house. The place was immaculate, the air scented with floral potpourri.

12

The two shelves that held books and toys and the school photograph – three smiling faces with well-brushed hair – were the only clues that the place was inhabited by children.

How do people do that? Are they perpetually cleaning? Wiping up sticky finger marks, hoovering up crumbs and crisps, sorting toys . . . or do they somehow train their children to be neat, tidy, clean and careful – in other words, to behave completely unlike children. How?

I'd long since reached an uneasy truce, accepting, against all the lessons my mother had drummed into me, that a basic level of mess and grime came with the territory. Life was messy, kids were messy, there were more important things than a clean swing bin. Now and then, when I could no longer bear the jumble in the toy boxes or the layers of food particles and felt-pen marks on the door-jamb and the television, I'd have a binge. It would look OK (never pristine, I could never do pristine) for an hour or two until it got lived in again.

Somehow Debbie had got it cracked. I sat opposite her on one of a pair of winged armchairs, drew out my note-book and began my enquiry.

I established her full name, her home situation (divorced, living alone here with three children), her place of work. She was a bit like her house, neat and trim. She was dressed in a fuchsia-pink ribbed sweater and a black skirt. Her hair was dark blonde, pulled into a low bun at the nape of her neck. She wore a little make-up, a silver cross on a chain, silver studs in her ears. 'Well turned out' was the phrase. She looked good but her hands trembled as she spoke and at times she became breathless and stumbled over her words.

I asked her to tell me about the man who had been following her. When had it started?

'It was about three months ago, just after Easter. I came out of work and he was there across the road. The

13

first couple of times I thought he was waiting to meet someone.'

'But you noticed him, you were aware of him?'

She played with her chain. 'He was staring at me longer than you normally do. Then he started to follow me.'

'From work?'

She nodded. 'He'd walk behind me, not close but in sight. Follow me to the bus stop. I . . . it wasn't . . . I didn't like it. One day I went to get Jason's birthday present,' she motioned to the photograph, 'and he was behind me. That's when it got to me, because I was sure he was actually doing it. There wasn't any doubt any more.'

'Was he there every day?'

'No. Sometimes he'd do two days in a row and then nothing for a few days then he'd turn up again.'

'No particular pattern?'

She thought for a moment, shook her head.

'Do you work every day?'

'No, I do Wednesday, Thursday and Saturdays, sometimes an extra day if one of the girls is sick or there's stocktaking.'

'Did you tell anyone at work about it?'

'Yeah, they all knew. Jean, that's the manageress, she went and had a word with him a couple of times, asked him to move on. He'd go off but he'd be there again when I came out, or I'd see him on the way to the bus. It just went on and on.' Her composure broke. 'It's awful,' she protested, her face crumpling, 'I keep thinking it must be me, something I've said or done. Why is he doing this?'

'You don't know him?'

'No, I've no idea who he is.'

'Does he seem at all familiar? Someone you might have met and forgotten?'

'No, I'm pretty good with faces. I've never seen him, I'm sure.'

'Has he ever spoken to you, approached you?'

'Not then but later.'

'Go on.'

'About a month after it had all started, I'd had enough. It's so . . .' she paused, finding the right word, running her thumb along the chain and back. 'It's creepy, it becomes the most important thing, it gets in the way of everything else.' She took a breath and exhaled slowly. 'So, I went up to him, at the bus stop. I told him to leave me alone, to stop following me or I'd report him to the police.'

She swallowed, opened her mouth to speak but couldn't. She ducked her head. When she did speak, it was a whisper; I strained to catch it. 'He knew my name.' She looked up and repeated herself, her voice breaking, high with panic. 'He knew my name. "Debbie," he said, that really freaked me out. How did he know my name?' she cried out.

I waited.

' "Don't be like this," he said, "you know how much you mean to me." ' She blushed. 'It was awful. "I love you," he said. "You know that." I couldn't stand it. I just ran then, to the bus. The next day this letter came, pages and pages of stuff about how much I meant to him and how long he'd waited to find me, on and on.' She shook her head in disbelief.

'Have you got the letter?'

'No, it made me feel dirty. I chucked it. There was no address or anything. It was posted in Manchester.'

'Was it signed?'

'Just the initial, G. There've been others since. I realized I'd better keep them, for evidence.' She rose and crossed to a wall cupboard and pulled out a large manila envelope. From inside it she took a bundle of letters. Thick, inky script, closely written. I read two and learned nothing other than that the writer G was obsessed with Debbie, was convinced they would eventually be together and live happily ever after. The language was clichéd and sentimental.

I also noticed there was no specific references in them, no mention of other people, of Debbie's children, no places and nothing that gave any clue to the writer's identity. It was all generalities like a badly written gift card going on for six pages at a time. The paper and envelopes were cheap – the sort sold at bargain discount outlets.

'Are they all like this?'

'Yes.'

'Can I keep a couple?'

'You can have the lot as far as I'm concerned,' she said bitterly. 'I can't stand having them in the house.'

'OK,' I said. 'I can keep them somewhere safe, they may be useful evidence.' She passed me the large envelope. 'Mrs Henderson says he's been here too.'

'Yes, just the last three weeks. That's when I went to the police. They said there was nothing they could do, that there's no law against it. But they said I could see a lawyer, maybe try getting some evidence of harassment.'

'When has he been here? Day or night?'

'Both. The first time, Sunday it was, I was taking the children to church. He was across the road by the alley, leaning on that wall.'

I went over and looked through the nets. Almost directly opposite there was a cobbled alleyway between two terraces leading to the back alleys.

'I didn't let on, I didn't want the children to know. He'd gone when we came back. Then a few days later, the Tuesday it was, my Mum had come round for her tea. I rang for a taxi to take her back, and I kept looking out so we wouldn't miss it, and he was there. Just staring, watching the house.' She caught her breath. 'I asked Mum to stay and I called the police. They sent someone round but he'd gone by the time they arrived.'

'Was he driving?'

'I never saw a car.'

'Describe him to me.'

16

I made notes as she spoke. Medium height, slim build, dark hair thinning on top, curly round the edges. Clean-shaven. Wears suit, neither flash nor ancient. Slightly out of date, ordinary dark suit, shirt, tie. Carries black umbrella. Age early thirties? Hard to tell.

'Has he spoken to you again?'

'Sometimes he calls out after me; sometimes he gets on the bus.' She chewed on her chain. 'It's awful,' she blurted out, 'I can't stand him. I just want him to go away. I've never done anything to him – why's he doing this to me?'

I'd no answers, only more questions. 'Has he ever threatened you?'

She shook her head. 'But the whole thing is threatening,' she complained. 'It's as if he's hunting me, getting closer all the time . . .' there was panic in her voice.

Stalking, that's the word they use. The man pursuing Debbie was a stalker.

'It must be terrible,' I agreed quietly, 'and you're obviously very frightened. It is a frightening situation. What we need to do now is gather evidence; if we can get some clear proof, it'll help the police even if it can't actually go to court. They might be able to scare him off. You've already got the letters, now we need to keep a record of everything else, so we can show the level of harassment he's subjecting you to. The next time you see him, ring me, no matter what time it is. If I can come I will.' I gave her my card and wrote my home number on the reverse. 'Try this number if the answerphone's on or I don't answer the mobile.'

'What will you do?'

'I'll take photos, maybe even use video, and I'll follow him – find out where he lives and who he is.'

She saw me to the door. I motioned to the array of locks and bolts. 'You've made the house secure – that's good. But he's not likely to hurt you,' I tried to reassure her. 'I realize it's an awful strain but it's very unlikely he'll use violence against you.'

'I know,' she said, 'that's what Mrs Henderson told me. But it doesn't change what it feels like. I'm really scared; he's hurting me already, it's messing my life up.' I could hear that panic again. Then she whispered: 'I'm so frightened.'

Yeah, so would I be, I thought, and I would take great satisfaction in running the little creep to ground.

CHAPTER THREE

'Mummy,' Maddie stood in the kitchen doorway, hands on her hips. 'There's a gigantic slug in the sandpit.'

'Is there?' I emptied the washing machine. Too late to peg it all out now but the forecast for the morning looked promising.

'Come and get it out now.'

'And slug poo,' Tom shouted from outside.

'It's nearly bedtime,' I warned them.

I scooped the brown and orange slug onto a trowel. It shrunk to a glistening lump of muscle and I dropped it into one of the beer traps I'd got dotted round the garden. At Tom's insistence I removed the slug poo too and put that on the soil.

While Maddie carefully sculpted a mermaid's house in the sand I wandered round dead-heading the pansies and the petunias, tidying up the tubs and baskets. Tom trundled the toy wheelbarrow round after me. Although there was only a year between Tom who was four, and Maddie, five going on six, he was still very much a little boy, short and stocky, hardly more than a toddler, while Maddie, in the midst of a growth spurt, looked lanky and skinny. Her body had assumed the proportions of a child now and she scorned anything she regarded as babyish.

It took me an hour and a half to get them both bathed, dressed and into bed, stories told and books read.

Ray was out. He'd gone for a drink with some of his fellow students from the computer course he's doing at Salford University. He earns his living as a joiner but he wants a change. He says he's had enough of manual labour and lousy working conditions.

It was barely warm enough to sit out but it was light and dry. And after all, this was the only summer we'd get. I put on an old fleecy top, found a blanket and the book I was reading, and fetched a lager from the fridge.

There was a clear sky, blue fading to apricot in the west. I leant my head back and watched the planes climbing out of Manchester Airport. Their trails criss-crossed in the sky, the white lines etched onto the blue, like ink bleeding on wet paper.

I hankered to be up there heading for somewhere hot with dusty roads and the scent of pink trees baking in the sun. I read and sipped my drink. As dusk fell I could no longer read the print. I yawned and stretched, gathered up my things. Weary again. It hadn't been a particularly gruelling day, but what with work and chores and children, every day was busy enough to tire me out.

I let Digger out in case Ray was late back. As I waited on the doorstep while he sniffed round the front garden I thought of Debbie Gosforth. Afraid to open the door, afraid to look out of the window. Was G stalking her tonight?

First thing Tuesday morning I got a call at the office. The man introduced himself as Victor Wallace; his son Luke was on remand in Golborne Remand Centre. He'd been arrested and charged with the murder of Ahktar Khan. The case had been committed for trial. 'You probably saw it in the papers. He didn't do it,' Mr Wallace said emphatically. 'They were mates, good friends, there's no way . . . I want you to talk to people – someone must have seen something. The place was busy, the club was emptying.'

I'd nothing more than vague recollections of the crime. 'When was it?' I stalled.

'First of January. It was the New Year's Eve party at Nirvana.'

The club was famous for its dance scene. People travelled from all over Europe for a night in Nirvana.

'And the police have charged him?'

'Murder. They've made up their minds. It's all a terrible mistake.'

'What about Luke's lawyer?'

'He knows I'm not happy, I want more doing. They've had people looking into it but they've not come up with anything very useful, nothing that'll clear him.'

Fragments of the story surfaced as I listened. There'd been talk of a racial motive. Luke Wallace was white; Ahktar Khan, an Asian Muslim, had been stabbed. And there had been something about Ecstasy. I wanted to know a lot more before I committed myself. I explained to Mr Wallace that he'd have to pay for my time, if I decided to take the case. Legal Aid was available for murder cases, but only to the official defence solicitor and people employed by them.

'Whatever it takes,' he insisted. 'I don't want to see Luke's life ruined for something he didn't do. I'll sell the house, the business, whatever.'

Crikey, I wasn't that expensive.

'We'd better meet,' I said, 'I need more information before I know whether I can help.'

'This afternoon?'

'Yes, early afternoon.' I had to pick up Maddie and Tom from school at three thirty, it didn't half eat into my working days.

He gave me an address in Prestwich. I told him I'd be there at half past one.

I was late. Prestwich is the other side of town from Withington and the traffic was all diverted round the bombed area. It was chaos. We edged slowly along Deansgate, where most of the shop fronts were boarded up; nothing was open. When we got to the bottom of Deansgate I peered up towards the Arndale and Marks & Spencers. In spite of seeing the images on television, I was still affected by the extent of the damage. My stomach clenched uneasily and I could feel tears not far away as I caught glimpses of twisted metal and shattered concrete, of Venetian blinds dangling broken from office windows and fractured lamp posts.

They were big houses, detached, each one a little different from its neighbour, with Tudor-style facades and leaded windows. Double-garage-and-gardener territory.

The Wallace house was at the end of the cul de sac. Beyond were trees and the sound of running water. The River Irwell came through here. The day was warm, sunny, the birds were in full throat. How nice it would be to just slip away, saunter through the trees to a sunny glade and watch the river flow, lose myself in the glistening reflections. As if.

A woman wearing a stripy butcher's apron opened the door. Unruly black hair, a bright expression.

'I've an appointment with Mr Wallace, Sal Kilkenny.'

'Oh, yes. Come on in. He's in the back.'

I followed her through the house, which was furnished like an Ikea showroom, to a large room at the back. One end with desk, shelves and PC obviously served as a study or office while the other half of the room was an open-plan lounge with television and sofas. Floor-length blinds occupied most of the far wall; they were shut but the translucent material allowed plenty of light in. I could see the shadowed outline of patio doors on the blinds. The place was cluttered and untidy but not dirty.

Victor Wallace rose from the desk as we came in, and stretched out his hand. His handshake was warm, firm.

'Thank you, Megan,' he said.

'Will you have tea?' the woman asked me, 'or coffee?'

'Thank you, coffee would be great.'

'Victor?'

22

'No, thanks.'

She left us.

'Please, sit down.' He gestured to the sofas, placed at right angles to each other. I opted for the firmest-looking one; there's nothing worse than trying to be businesslike while sliding inexorably into a horizontal position on a soggy sofa. He took the other.

He gave off a palpable air of restless energy. Frustration, even. He was a stocky man with small, square hands, a round, shiny face as though someone had polished him, receding hairline, grey hair. He wore jeans, a casual sweatshirt but good quality. Chicago Bears on the front.

'What I'd like to do,' I began, 'is ask you some initial questions, get the overall picture of what's happened, both about Ahktar Khan's death and since.'

He nodded briskly.

'Let's start with New Year's Eve.'

He spoke so rapidly it was all I could do to note the essential facts, but that was all right at this stage. I could go over any gaps later if I decided to take the job. What I needed now was the flavour of the case. It would help me to establish whether there was anything that made me uneasy or rang alarm bells, whether there was any point in Mr Wallace paying me, or if I was a last-ditch attempt to do something in a hopeless situation.

Luke and Ahktar and two other friends had gone to Nirvana for the big New Year's Eve bash. The boys were close friends from school; they had formed a band and used to practise in the Wallaces' basement.

Victor knew Luke would be home late, so he'd made sure he had plenty of cash for a taxi.

Where was Mrs Wallace in all this? Was there one? I'd ask later.

At five he was woken by a phone call from the duty solicitor at the police station. Luke was being held for questioning in connection with an affray.

They didn't tell him any more over the phone.

'I thought it was a mix-up – you know, some horseplay got out of hand – though frankly, even that surprised me.'

'Why?'

'Luke's not like that. He's never been in a fight in his life, hates practical jokes,' he smiled. 'It wasn't cool, you see. At that age, it's all image, isn't it, and Luke and Ahktar, they were into being grown-up. They'd no time for kids' stuff.'

He'd waited for two and half hours at the police station before he'd found out that Ahktar was dead as a result of an assault with a knife, and that Luke was being questioned about the incident.

'I couldn't believe it,' he said. 'He was a lovely boy – bright, friendly – he and my son were inseparable. It seemed ludicrous that he was dead.' He paused, remembering something else, shifted on the sofa. 'And I thought: Thank God, it's not Luke. I hated myself for thinking that.' He took a deep breath, wiped his hands on his jeans.

'So, I waited and waited, hours on end. It was so difficult to find out what was happening. They kept telling me to go home, they expected me to walk away and leave him there. I couldn't understand why they were being so brutal. His friend was dead – surely it wouldn't take all day to establish what Luke had seen! I thought he was a witness, you see,' he still spoke quickly, his voice tight with frustration and pent-up energy. 'In the end I blew up at the guy on the desk. Finally they sent someone to talk to me. He tells me that Luke is a suspect, that they think he may have killed Ahktar. I laughed, it was so preposterous. I told them no way, there was some horrific mistake, they were best friends.'

There was a knock at the door and Megan came in with a tray, coffee in a little cafetière, milk and sugar, shortbread biscuits. She set it down on the table near to me. As Mr Wallace thanked her, something in the way he said it told me that they weren't friends or relatives but that she worked for him.

'They said he hadn't been fit to interview when they'd brought him in and they were waiting to question him in the morning. It must have been mid morning by then, you lose all track of time. They held him all that day, and the next. They kept going to the magistrates to get another twenty-four hours. I saw him for ten minutes, twice in all that time. Then they charged him.' He covered his mouth and looked away.

I occupied myself pouring the coffee. The bitter aroma filled the room. I ate a biscuit. He got to his feet and crossed to the blinds, pressed a switch at the side; they glided back.

'Oh,' I said softly. Beyond lay a stunning garden, shaped by clumps of bamboo and various conifers. There were two apple trees at one corner, an alpine rockery and a large pool. Old York flagstone paths connected the different areas and the lush grass was dotted with daisies and clover. I got to my feet for a better look. 'It's beautiful,' I said. It was so unlike the traditional clipped lawns and standard roses I'd seen in the neighbours' front gardens. Most of the planting was green or architectural, and there was little of the annual colour with which I stuffed my own pots and window-boxes. The colours in the rockery were muted – white, soft pink, here and there a tiny flash of a stronger red or purple, but there was a restraint to it all. Beside the pool a boulder had been placed. It was perfect.

'Yes, it is beautiful,' Mr Wallace replied. 'Do you garden?'

'A bit,' I said, overawed by the comparison.

'Glenda, my wife, designed it. Place was full of hydrangeas and gladioli when we moved in. She died,' he carried on, 'six years ago now. We keep it just as she made it. We could sit outside if you . . .'

'Yes.'

'I'll get the key.' He strode over to his desk and came back with a bunch of keys. He unlocked the French windows. I gathered up my tray and book and we settled on seats on the patio immediately next to the house.

'So,' he resumed his story, 'I asked to see the person in charge. They made me wait, of course. I told him they'd got the wrong person. I explained how close the boys were, that neither of them got into fights. That Luke would never hurt Ahktar. The man listened, he thanked me, he said nothing. As far as I can see, they've got a suspect and they want to make it fit.'

'But without proof . . .'

'Apparently they have two witnesses.'

CHAPTER FOUR

Driving back through the city centre was even slower than getting there. I felt exhausted by meeting Mr Wallace and the intensity of his emotional state. I had an image I couldn't shift of the knife in Ahktar's chest. I don't like knives. I was stabbed once. *Please don't*, I'd begged. *He raised his arm . . . the knife shining . . .* No. I shook the memories away.

My shoulder was stiff and aching. I rolled it back round and round as I queued up to get onto Princess Street. We inched forward a couple of cars at a time when the lights changed, but the traffic ahead was hardly moving. There'd been a crash. I crawled past wanting to avert my eyes, needing to look. A woman in one of the cars had a neck brace on. She was being lifted out by two ambulance men. I sighed with relief; no blood, no dead bodies or worse, no decapitated driver or twitching limbs imprinted on my mind for the rest of my life.

If Ahktar had been stabbed outside the club as everyone was coming out, surely there would have been more than two witnesses? There'd have been blood, a skirmish; people would have glanced, looked, stared. There would have been the unmistakable atmosphere of violence, the scent of danger and death that we all recognize instinctively, that speeds up our heartbeat and raises the hairs on the back of our neck. I needed to find some of those witnesses. Six months after the event it wouldn't be easy, and acting for the defence we could hardly get a slot on Crimewatch to pull people in. I'd start with the list Mr Wallace had given me, but from what he'd said none of the witnesses had come up with anything substantial the defence could use. Before I talked to anyone though, I'd book a visit to Golborne and meet Luke, assess for myself whether I thought he was wrongly accused. As an independent operator I had the freedom to choose who I worked for and what the terms were, and I'd said to Mr Wallace that I would only take the case if I felt comfortable working for Luke's release.

Sheila rang. They were reopening Victoria Station so she hoped to travel home the following day. The news continued to be dominated by the bomb. Television and newspapers featured devastating pictures of the Arndale Centre and surrounding buildings; the gaping windows, twisted metal and fragments of concrete. It still made my stomach churn. Much was made of the bridge that linked Marks & Spencers with the Arndale Centre. It had literally jumped several feet in the air with the force of the blast, yet had fallen back into place in one piece – albeit unsafe. And a red pillar box close to the centre of the blast had inexplicably survived while everything about it was smashed to smithereens.

There were tales of folly and bravery, of interrupted weddings and miraculous escapes. Hundreds of people were still unable to get to work, to visit their businesses, retrieve their cars, return to their homes. I read it all.

On page eight a headline caught my eye. MYSTERY WOMAN AT BELLE VUE SUICIDE SCENE. I recalled the look of shock on Mrs Grady's face, the ominous sound of flies busy at the corpse.

Local resident, Mrs Grady, 62, claimed she'd been alerted by a mystery caller. 'She wouldn't say who she was or what she was doing there. She wouldn't have her photograph taken. I thought that was a bit odd at the time.

I'd no idea who she was. She left as soon as she could.' I groaned. They'd had to put a spin on it. Rather than just relate the facts of Mr Kearsal's death they'd spiced it up with a whiff of intrigue.

Mr Kearsal, 68, was found hanging at his Belle Vue home on the evening of Thursday June 13th. He had not been seen since the previous Thursday. Mr Kearsal, who lived alone, leaves a sister in Harrogate. At this stage police do not suspect foul play; a note was found at the scene.

It was a non-story. Of course the police knew who I was, and a call to them from the reporter would have established that immediately, unless the police were being awkward about it. I groaned again. All I needed was some bright, bored reporter determined to uncover my identity, and the whole thing could blow out of all proportion. Local notoriety would be disastrous for my business. I needed my anonymity.

I could see it now. PRIVATE EYE HOUNDS BROKEN MAN. IS THIS WOMAN ON YOUR TAIL?

I hoped to God it would fade away.

I'd just topped up the bath for myself when I heard the phone. I let Ray answer it, hoping it would be for him. Wrong.

'It's Debbie Gosforth,' her voice said, high with strain. 'He's here now, across the street.'

Shit.

'Can you come?' She was breathless.

'Yes. Listen, I won't come to the house – that might alert him – but I'll wait down the street and try to follow him when he goes. What's he wearing?'

'His suit. He's by the alley, where I showed you.'

'How long's he been there?'

'I don't know. I only saw him just now when I went to close the curtains upstairs. He wasn't there earlier.'

'I've got a mobile phone,' I said. 'I can ring you to let

you know when he leaves. Stay inside. Try and keep your phone clear.'

I hate working evenings and nights but it can't be avoided when surveillance is involved. The call can come anytime. And apart from my personal reluctance, nights are actually easier to arrange than earlier in the day because I can usually rely on Ray being there for the children.

After school can be very tricky, and on more than one occasion I've had to take the children with me. They're good camouflage for short periods. Who suspects a woman with two children of being an investigator? But they are definitely time-limited as far as eating crisps and playing I-Spy in a stationary car goes.

I pulled the plug on the bath then checked with Ray and left details of where I was going.

'Nothing risky, is it?' he asked.

'No. Someone else is being stalked; all I need to do is tail him home when he's had enough. Long as I make sure he doesn't cotton on, I'll be fine.'

It was almost dark now, the streetlights turning from red to orange. I could feel excitement building as I drove west towards Chorlton. Surveillance is mind-numbing, utterly, crunchingly boring, but the prospect of seeing this guy, of hiding from him and tailing him sent shivers of anticipation through me. Like a kid playing hide-and-seek.

I was there in quarter of an hour. I wasn't sure where my best vantage point would be, and as he was on foot he could walk off in either direction. I cruised slowly down Debbie's road. Both sides were lined with cars which could be a help or a hindrance. I looked quickly at the alley as I passed but couldn't see him. I drove round the block and passed again. No man in a suit. I parked round the corner and rang Debbie's.

'Debbie, it's Sal Kilkenny. I'm round the corner but I can't see him by the alley. Have a look out, will you?'

There was a clatter as she put the phone down and a pause before she returned.

'He's gone,' she said, 'I'm sorry.'

'No, you were right to call me.'

'He was there,' she sounded upset, 'he was, I didn't imagine it.'

'It's all right,' I said, 'I believe you. This sort of thing happens all the time. You weren't to know how long he'd be there. Does he ever come back? Come and go, sort of thing?'

'No.'

'He's not likely to come back tonight, then?'

'I don't think so.'

'Ring me if he does. Are you OK? I could pop in for a few minutes?'

'No, I'm fine. I've only just got Connor to sleep, his asthma's bad. He'd be up again if he heard the door.'

'Well, ring me as soon as you see him again, day or night.'

'Yeah. OK. G'night.'

I felt deflated. The prospect of bed rather than hours getting cramp in the car was welcome but it was as if I'd been cheated. My adrenalin had kicked in and had no part to play. I'd need a good hour to let it subside. At home I prowled around. There was nothing on television (again), I tried reading but found I'd reached the bottom of the page with questions about the stalker weaving through my mind.

I wandered into the kitchen to make a drink. I could hear the murmur of the radio from the cellar below where Ray has his carpentry workshop. He makes furniture with great love and skill and absolutely no commercial acumen. For money he works as a joiner for some local builders. They contact him when they get a big job on and he works like mad for a month or so, and then has to catch up on his computer course. But the carpentry is where his soul is.

31

The hob was filthy. I ran hot water and picked up the pan scrub and the cream cleaner.

An hour later the hob, oven, work surface and kettle were gleaming. The rest of the room was still cluttered but as I said I don't do pristine. Besides, I'd unwound enough to go to bed.

CHAPTER FIVE

I'd come away from Victor Wallace's with the names and addresses of Luke's friends, including the Khan family, the lawyer's details and a sketchy list of who had been visited and interviewed by the defence solicitor or people acting for him.

I'd also got the visiting details for Golborne, the place in East Lancashire where Luke was being held. It made sense to start by seeing him first and then the others who'd been interviewed. I'd rung and arranged a visit as soon as I'd got home on the Tuesday after seeing Mr Wallace. They'd booked me in for the Friday morning.

I duly reported to the visitor's centre adjacent to the remand centre the following afternoon.

Golborne Remand Centre is newer than either Risley or Hindley and boasts a better safety record – fewer suicides. It was one of the first places to be run by Group 4 Security, and when it opened there was a blaze of publicity, mostly about the adjoining Young Offender's Institution which was to be run like a boot camp along American lines. Never mind that all the statistics show such regimes fail to turn around most young offenders.

Just getting near the place made me want to abscond. The idea of being locked up terrified me, not only because of the loss of liberty but because of the enforced separation from Maddie. She'd be taken into care, devastated. I'd lose her.

I shook away the frightening fantasies. I was checked through an electronic door, a bit like the ones at airports. The visitors' lounge was awash with children and thick with smoke. There was a drinks machine in the corner. I was shown to a table and waited for them to take me through to see Luke Wallace.

Ten minutes later, suffering seriously from the effects of passive smoking, I was collected by a guard. He carefully unlocked the door through from the lounge and locked it behind us before using his keys on the next one. We walked down a narrow windowless corridor and then passed through another secured lobby leading into a longer corridor with a row of enclosed booths along one wall. I was shown to one of the cubicles. It had a small table and two chairs placed opposite each other. One wall was clear from waist height so we could be observed by the guards.

'I'll bring him through now, miss.' The guard went, leaving the door shut but not locked.

A sign in large black capitals instructed all visitors not to pass any materials to prisoners, and warned that all materials including gifts e.g. cigarettes and food must be checked through the main office.

Although the place was only a few years old it already bore the marks of interminable time. The floor and walls and even the furniture were pocked with cigarette burns. The place stank of stale nicotine. There were names and dates scratched on the paintwork, and the see-through partition was a mass of scratches. I shifted in my seat trying to get comfortable, tried to edge my chair forward. I couldn't. It was bolted to the floor.

Luke Wallace had the same stocky frame as his father though he was much slimmer, and the same round face. His thick hair was cut with a wedge in the back and fell to his eyes at the front in a heavy fringe.

He sat down and folded his hands on the table in front of him.

'Just give us a nod when you're finished,' the guard said. He left the room, locking it behind him.

I introduced myself and explained what his father wanted me to do. As I spoke he kept looking away, studying his hands or staring over at the notice on the wall then casting sideways glances at me.

At first I mistook it for teenage disaffection, a show of boredom or restlessness then, as he glanced my way once more, I saw that he was scared witless. He couldn't meet my eyes because he'd become cowed, disturbed by the nightmare he was living. He'd lost all confidence; he no longer knew who he could trust. In an effort to reassure him I repeated that his father had employed me.

'Luke, I want you to tell me about Ahktar – anything, everything.'

'I can't remember.'

'No, not about New Year's Eve, before that. You were friends,' I prompted.

'Yes.'

'Did you go to the same primary school?'

'No,' he shook his head, 'secondary. We were in the same class, did the same subjects. We both stayed on . . .' He broke off. The world of A levels and the sixth form common room a million miles away.

'Your dad said you were good friends.'

He nodded, chewed a corner of his lip, sat very still. 'I didn't do it,' he said quietly, and his nose grew red and his eyes shone. He swallowed, struggled hard for composure.

'But you don't remember,' I said gently.

He took a breath. 'I never . . . he was my best . . .' His efforts failed and tears streamed down his cheeks. He put his hands up to cover his face. I glanced over at the window. Would they yank him away for so emotional a display? I reached across and put my hand on Luke's shoulder. He cried almost silently, his head bobbing in his hands.

Indignation flared in me. This boy, barely a man, hadn't

35

been tried yet, might well be innocent – but he was in here alone and terrified almost senseless. I shouldn't think he'd have had any access to counselling, or seen anyone to help him deal with the trauma he'd been through. If he fell apart they'd put him in the hospital, but until then . . .

After what seemed like ages he straightened up. I withdrew my hand; my arm had gone dead and I rubbed at it to stop the pins and needles while he wiped his face with the palms and backs of his hands. I passed him some tissues. *Do not pass any materials to the prisoner.* He blew his nose noisily.

The crying had calmed him. His eyes no longer swept here and there. He gazed steadily into the distance. 'They wouldn't let me go to the funeral. I should have been there.' He looked directly at me, 'I still can't believe he's dead. I dream about him and then I wake up and . . .' He sighed. 'When we were in Year Seven, that's when my mum died, Ahktar, he was great. He didn't mind if I got moody or anything, he just stuck with me. There was no one else. My dad was in a right state. Ahktar was . . . he didn't talk about it or anything,' he leant forward, trying to make me understand, 'he just kept coming round. He wasn't embarrassed, everybody . . . that's the main thing, they're embarrassed, they make you feel awkward.' He paused. 'We've still got his guitar in the cellar.'

'You had a group? What instrument did you play?'

'Drums, Ahktar on guitar and vocals, Simon on bass, Josh on keyboards. Ahktar made it though.' He smiled at some memory; it made him look so young. 'He had a brilliant voice and he wrote the songs as well. That night, New Year's Eve, we were going to see this guy at the club. He had a recording studio, his brother was one of the DJs at the club. Ahktar had talked to the DJ and he said he'd introduce us.'

'Did he?'

'Nah. It was crazy in there.'

'So you do remember part of the evening?'

'Yeah, we got the bus into town, we went straight there. Everyone knew it'd sell out. We were there by eight. We all got in.'

'Who were you with?'

'Simon, Josh and his girlfriend, Ahktar, Joey D, Zeb and Emma.'

I asked him about the people who hadn't been mentioned before.

'Joey D.' He shook his head slowly. 'Joey D is sad. He's at school with us. He has a hard time, his old man's an alcoholic. Joey lives with his grandma. She's loaded, rolling in it. Joey's got more money than sense, so people use him. He gives them stuff, he thinks they'll like him.'

'What sort of stuff?'

He shrugged. 'CDs, computer games, watches.'

'Drugs?'

'Maybe.' Automatic caution.

I stared at Luke. 'Listen, Luke . . .'

'OK,' he said. I didn't need to finish my little speech about complete honesty. Luke recognized his mistake.

'Yeah, he could get most things – dope, E, whizz.'

'For you?'

'Sometimes, for parties, not on a regular basis. Well, only dope as a regular thing.'

'Did you all smoke dope?'

'Yeah.'

'And the rest? Whizz, E?'

'Yeah, the weekend or parties like I said. Everyone does it, it's not a problem.'

I nodded. 'OK, so Joey D was there. Who else?'

'Zeb, Ahktar's cousin, and Emma.'

'He's at school with you?'

He smiled briefly. 'No, he's older, he works for his brother Janghir. They all call him Jay. Clothing business. They've a place up Cheetham Hill.'

'And when you got inside, what did you do?'

He thought about it. 'We went to the big room downstairs. We had a drink. We had a dance. It was livening up. Zeb had brought Ahktar this jacket he'd been after for ages. Canadian import, can't get them here. Really nice jacket, silk and microfibre, black and yellow. Weighs nothing, really warm. They use them up in the Arctic. Anyway Zeb has one and Ahktar had paid him cash up front back in the summer. It was getting hot but Ahktar, he won't take this jacket off.' He smiled. 'Everyone took a tab. Everyone was dancing.'

'Who did you get it from?'

'Joey. He'd gone off to sort it soon as we got in there.'

'Go on.'

'That's it. There was lots of stuff going round – pills, some heavy dope. Everyone was trying it all.'

'Including you?'

He nodded. 'I can't remember anything else, not till . . . after. Someone said they were going to turn the sprinklers on at midnight, cool everyone down for New Year but I think that was just a rumour.'

'Do you remember leaving the club?'

'No.'

'Do you remember anything outside the club?'

'I've tried, there's nothing.'

'Do you remember going to the police station?'

He studied his hands. 'No. The next thing I knew I was waking up, I was cold, I was shaking. There was blood all over my T-shirt and my hands. I thought I'd had a nosebleed.' He looked at me. 'It wasn't my blood, it was Ahktar's. They asked me all these questions then. I couldn't tell them anything. They just kept on about Ahktar, what had we argued about? I couldn't remember anything. In the end, I lost it. I shouted at him: "I can't fucking remember! Why don't you ask Ahktar?" One of them stared at me, hard. "We can't," he said, "he's dead." '

I spent another half hour talking to Luke, going over

details, checking names and addresses. I asked him about motives, too – who might have wanted to kill his friend? He hadn't a clue. Ahktar was bright, popular but not cocky. He used drugs for fun like they all did, but he wasn't involved in anything criminal. He was an ordinary eighteen-year-old studying for A levels, playing in a band. Just like Luke who was now accused of murder.

Before I left I took him back to the night at the club and asked him to think again of anything he could remember – familiar faces, funny moments, anything. He began to shake his head then hesitated.

'Emma, Zeb's girlfriend, she left early. They'd fallen out, I think.'

'Was that unusual?'

'No, Zeb is a bit of a . . .' I watched Luke struggle to find a word but there was only one would do.

'Wanker?' I supplied.

He blushed slightly. 'Yeah, he goes to the casino, spends a fortune, then he's borrowing. He'd borrow off Emma and she'd get really pissed off. She's a nursery nurse, he makes more in a week than she earns in a month. Anyway, she went. And then I saw Zeb, looks like he's giving Joey D a hard time.'

'Borrowing money?'

'I don't know. I couldn't hear, you couldn't hear a thing unless someone yelled in your ear. But Zeb had Joey D by the collar and then Joey goes upstairs.'

'At the time what did you think?'

'Nothing. Well, Joey can be a pain and I thought Zeb was fed up because Emma had gone and maybe he was taking it out on Joey D. He never knows when to keep a low profile.'

'Could it have been about drugs? You said Joey had supplied the stuff that night.'

'Dunno. Maybe. Zeb was well into toot – cocaine,' he added for my benefit.

'Did he get it from Joey?'

He shrugged. 'Don't think so. Just something Ahktar said one time about how much he spent on it and how miserable he still was.'

'But Joey could have got it for him?'

'Oh, yeah. Joey'd do anything if he thought it got him in with you. He's like a little kid really.'

I asked Luke what he'd been told of the sequence of events that night – or what had been implied by the police and the prosecution.

He blew a breath out, shifted in his seat. 'They reckon I stabbed him. Outside the club, there's a small alley behind the side entrance, there's bins there. That's where they found us. Together,' he whispered. 'It's quiet round there. The taxis and that, the buses, town – it's all in the other direction.'

'Who found you?'

'Dunno, someone rang an ambulance, don't know who. It was too late for Ahktar.'

'Were you awake?'

'No, they couldn't rouse me.'

'And the witnesses they've got?'

He pressed his hands onto his knees and swayed in the chair 'They saw me and Ahktar fighting, shouting, they say I had a knife. They say I stabbed him.' He spaced out his words, trying to hold himself together. 'I didn't,' he insisted, 'I didn't.'

But they identified him.

'Did you have a knife?'

'No,' he was emphatic, 'I've never carried a knife. They're saying I borrowed it or took it, it's like one Joey D had.'

'Could Joey have hurt Ahktar?'

'No, he's all mouth. He's no hard man. He'd run a mile.'

'The knife was there?'

He rolled his eyes back and blinked hard. 'It was still in

him – there was just one wound. My fingerprints were on the knife.'

Even worse. But there was more than one way to get prints on a knife – trying to remove it, for example.

Before I left I asked Luke to keep thinking about that night and stressed that if he remembered any other details, to tell me about them. I had left my card with reception, it would be given to Luke at an appropriate time, presumably once they'd checked it hadn't been soaked with hallucinogens.

I told him who I planned to talk to and made sure he had no objection to me asking my questions. I also asked him to consider hypnosis. His amnesia, probably due to the cocktail of drink and drugs he'd taken, was a terrible obstacle to his defence. And while information from somebody under hypnosis probably wouldn't be admitted in court, it could still help me to find witnesses to the crime and might even give a lead as to who'd stabbed Ahktar.

I knew it wasn't beyond the bounds of possibility for Luke to have done it, but then it wasn't beyond the bounds of possibility for me to win the Lottery. Except I don't buy tickets. I prefer to work with probabilities. And Luke probably didn't kill Ahktar. Someone else probably did, and they were escaping detection. The police had enough evidence to believe that a reasonable jury would find Luke guilty. The thought made me uneasy. Much of their case rested on the witnesses they'd got. It was vital I found out what they'd seen and established whether they could have been mistaken or whether I was up to my neck in a lost cause.

I stood up and went to the partition, motioned to the guard who was standing along the corridor.

'When you see his parents,' Luke said, 'will you tell them I'm sorry, tell them I didn't do it? They think I did. They wouldn't talk to my dad. Tell them.'

'I will.' If they'll talk to me, I added to myself.

CHAPTER SIX

Every set of lights on the East Lancs Road went red.
And there are many sets. I tried not to get tense but the
car was hot and my temples were starting to thump. I had
a raging thirst. I hadn't had a drink since breakfast and
the smoky air at the Centre had added to my dry mouth. I
pulled in at a garage, bought a bottle of mineral water and
glugged it all the way to town.

I drove round for almost half an hour before finding
a parking space. The cordon still barricaded off Cross
Street, Market Street and Cannon Street, and although
many of the buses and the Metro Link were now running,
the traffic flow through town was still at a snail's pace.

Manchester does have some beautiful buildings, and
the Central Library is one of them. Like a cross between
the Coliseum and the Parthenon, it's a delight in white
marble, albeit smeared with grey from the pollution. It has
large round pillars supporting the porch at the front and
repeated on a smaller scale around the dome and the upper
floors. The libraries inside are circular, light and airy from
the glass ceilings. And plastered with notices warning of
pickpockets and bag thieves.

I walked up the stairs to the Social Sciences library and
headed for the microfiche newspaper archives. The local
papers along with the national dailies were all there. I
sought out issues from just after New Year. There were no
local papers until 2nd of January. Coverage of the murder

42

of Ahktar Khan dominated the headlines. NEW YEAR STABBING TRAGEDY. Ahktar in a classic school-photo pose took up most of the front page. I read the reports, which were sketchy and speculative. I scrolled forward, winding the film on to the next front page. KHAN KILLING – POLICE DENY RACIAL MOTIVE and the next: SCHOOLBOY KILLING – SUSPECT HELD. Later in the week they proclaimed: KHAN MURDER – POLICE CHARGE SCHOOLFRIEND.

There was a picture of the two boys next to a drum kit with two friends. Their band.

I made photocopies of the relevant stories to take away. The papers had covered the murder for most of that week, but the speed with which they had charged Luke Wallace with the crime put an end to the press interest.

My mobile rang just as I got back to the car. I answered it and paced back around the car park, ducking and weaving in an effort to improve the reception. The phone crackled. 'Hello,' I shouted. 'Can you hear me?'

More static, then a couple of words. 'Sal . . . here.' Enough for me to recognize the voice of my best friend, Diane.

'Diane!' I yelled, hoping she could hear me. 'I'll ring you back.'

I walked round the corner and stood next to a wall; my mobile seemed to like walls. Diane answered, clear as a bell. 'I thought you meant later,' she said. 'Look, I can't make tomorrow, can we change it to Monday?'

I cast around for problems. Ray hadn't mentioned anything; he should be in. 'Fine.'

'Come for a meal?'

'What's the big occasion?' We usually met at a pub halfway between her house in Rusholme and mine in Withington.

'I fancy a good meal, I can't stretch to a restaurant, next best thing. What do you reckon?'

43

'Yes, love to.'

'Seven thirty?'

'Great.'

Teatime at home was a disaster. Maddie burst into tears and refused to eat a morsel. Something to do with the layout of the food on the plate. Tom had been fine until he knocked his blackcurrant juice all over his plate and the rest of the table. I struggled hard to force food down into my stomach which was tense with irritation. Maddie continued to howl until I told her to go off and do it somewhere else. She stormed off. Ray cast me a questioning look.

'I'm not in the mood,' I said. 'It drives me up the wall when she does this, when she won't explain what's wrong. God, if I knew she wanted the flipping peas in the middle I'd put them in the middle. I'm not telepathic.'

'You should be,' Ray said. 'It's a prerequisite of motherhood.'

The door flew open and Maddie flounced in. 'Mummy.' She'd stopped crying now and she was all outrage. 'You didn't give me any tea and I'll starve and I'll die and then you'll be really sorry and I'll be glad.' She wheeled round and pulled the door to behind her hard. She was trying for a satisfying slam. Unfortunately a well-placed stuffed dinosaur was in the way and the door merely bounced back open again.

I covered my mouth to stifle the giggles. It wasn't the first time she'd threatened me this way, but I reckoned her mouthing off her anger at me was probably healthier than swallowing it all and storing it up for adult life.

Of course by bedtime peace had been restored. We'd talked about my need to know about her constantly shifting requirements – not that I thought it would make one iota of difference. I hugged her, told her I loved her and read a long story. I even managed to bite my tongue when she complained of feeling hungry and brought her warm milk and an apple. Perfect mother or what?

I needed to make some sense of my notes while Luke's voice was still fresh in my mind. It was half past nine before I got a chance to sit down and work through them. Dusk was only just falling. Midsummer, 21st of June, the longest day of the year. I sat on the sofa with the curtains open and the small table-lamp on. I could see the back garden as I worked, and watch the night steal across from behind the trees at the end, the sky turning purple then navy.

It would save me a lot of time and Victor Wallace a lot of money if I could find out exactly what information Luke's solicitor had already gathered. I made a list of people to contact the following day and put them at the top. I'd got some names and addresses from both Victor Wallace and Luke – mainly the friends who had gone with them to the club on New Year's Eve.

'Tea?' Ray poked his head round the door.

'Yes, love one.'

He returned shortly with a mug for each of us and eased himself into the armchair.

'Work?'

'Yes.' I set aside my papers. 'I needed to get it down before it became lost among all the other rubbish floating round in here.' I tapped my head. 'I've done now.'

'Aah!' He started. 'Jonathan.'

'Eh?'

'Jonathan can come so that's eight.'

'Oh.' He was talking about Tom's birthday party – eight five-year-olds in hyperdrive for two hours. 'We can do it all outside if it's dry.'

'Yep, less jelly ground into the carpet.'

'Did you order a cake?'

'Sheila's offered to do one.'

'Brilliant.' Sheila, a mature student, rented our attic flat and so helped to keep the household solvent. She had moved to Manchester after her divorce. Her family had grown up and left home. Prior to her arrival, baking cakes had been accorded the status of a quaint historic tradition, like using the mangle or embroidering pillow cases. Interesting to know about, but not the sort of thing anybody did in real life any more. Birthday cakes were small round sponges from the local bakery with pastel icing in one of three designs – football shirt, clown or teddy. Reliable, dull, uninspired. And pricey.

'What will she do?'

'She thought about a dinosaur.'

'Oh, he'd love that.'

I heard the stairs creak and a small cough. 'Maddie?'

'I can't sleep, there's a thing in my room.'

'Come here.'

She came in looking miserable. 'And my head hurts.'

'That's probably because you're very tired.'

'I'm not.'

'Come on, we'll take you up, sort out this thing.'

The thing turned out to be a Blu-Tac mark which Maddie claimed looked like a witch. Not content with logical explanations, I ended up covering it with one of her paintings. I tucked her in and sang several verses of *'There's a hole in my bucket, dear Liza, dear Liza'*.

'I'll come up and check on you in a few minutes.'

'But it's still there, Mummy, under the picture.'

'I know, but you can't see it, can you?'

'I can in my thinking voice.'

'Oh, yes.' And short of repainting the whole flipping room there's nothing I can do about it. It'll be there for years so you'd better just get used to the idea. 'Now I'm going downstairs and I'll come up and check on you soon.' I tried not to snap.

'When?'

'In a few minutes.'

'How many?'

Count to ten. 'Fifteen minutes.'

'Fifteen minutes?' Horrified. 'That's ages!'

'OK, five.' There was no clock in her room so she'd not catch me out. I half-expected her to reappear but she didn't, and gradually I relaxed again as Ray and I continued to discuss the party plans. When I went up an hour later she was fast asleep on the floor beside her bed. Presumably Blu-Tac witches have less power at floor level.

CHAPTER SEVEN

Luke's solicitor, Dermott Pitt, had his practice in town off Deansgate, a few minutes' walk from the Metro station. It was far enough from the centre of the blast to have escaped damage. The renovated townhouses were all shiny wrought-iron railings and brass plaques, but inside there wasn't room to swing a cat.

Dermott Pitt had been able to fit me in between ten thirty and eleven – or, as his secretary put it, 'He has a ten-thirty window.' She'd been watching too many American television imports.

He and I sat either side of a solid dark wood desk with a leather blotter. The desk was far too big for the room. A ceiling fan turned slowly and silently above us.

'Ms Kilkenny,' he used the prefix effortlessly, 'you've been retained by Mr Victor Wallace to carry out investigations into the death of Ahktar Khan. Yes?'

'That's right.'

'You realize that I represent Luke Wallace and only Luke Wallace. He is my client, not his friends nor his family nor his next-door neighbour.' He stretched his lips in a parody of a smile. 'So?' he challenged me.

'Yes, I realize that but I took the trouble to ask Luke for his agreement that I talk to you, and I established that he would be happy for you to disclose any relevant details about the case. In confidence, of course.'

He looked a little sick. 'We have, as I'm sure you are

aware, made our own extensive enquiries,' he stalled, 'and I believe we have built up the best possible defence for my client. However . . .' he spread his hands. If I wished to waste everyone's time like this . . .

'It would help me,' I kept my voice even, 'if you could outline how you intend to defend the case, and in particular tell me what you have discovered regarding the witnesses. Their evidence seems to form the basis for the prosecution's case.'

Dermott Pitt looked most unhappy. His upper lip curled slightly. 'We intend to concentrate on the complete lack of motive, of intent, and the fact that there was no shred of evidence of ill will between the victim and the accused. The accused neither owned nor carried a knife, and he made no attempt to quit the scene. Quite the reverse.'

'And the witnesses?'

He shifted in his chair, ran a thumb along the edge of his desk. He pursed his lips. 'In my view and that of my learned colleagues, it is paramount that we introduce a degree of doubt into the veracity and accuracy of the witnesses' statements. The night was dark,' he gestured with his hand laying out the points of his argument for me, 'people may have been drinking or consuming illegal drugs, the witnesses may have confused the meaning of the scene they reported – an over-eager greeting can, for example, be misinterpreted as a violent assault. Then there is the question of their delay in coming forward. Why such a delay? And how would it impact on their recollection of events?'

'Delay?'

'They came forward late the following day.'

'So they didn't ring for the ambulance?'

'No,' he didn't elaborate.

'What did they do?'

'They returned home.'

'After witnessing a murder?' I was incredulous.

49

'It is an area we intend to probe in great depth.'

'But presumably the police—'

'The police are happy with the evidence the prosecution has, but we will be challenging that view.'

'I'd like to speak to the witnesses,' I said. 'I have their names already. Victor Wallace gave me all the information he had about who'd been seen.'

Pitt raised and lowered his eyebrows but kept his own counsel.

'If you have their addresses?'

He paused. I waited. I resisted the urge to justify my request, to reason and mollify. I sat tight. He switched on the intercom on his desk. 'Frances, get me the Wallace file, will you?'

'What about the weapon?' I asked. 'Have you any idea where that came from? Luke told me it resembled one that Joey Deason carried.'

'It did, but the police established that the Deason boy still had his.'

His secretary brought in the file and he took it from her. She closed the door softly behind her when she left. In neat italics he transcribed names and addresses using a fountain pen with blue ink onto thick embossed white paper. He blotted it carefully on his blotter. He'd have been completely at home in a costume drama, Dickens or Austen.

He held the paper between his fingers just out of my reach. A carrot on a stick. 'Ms Kilkenny, please proceed with the utmost discretion. Any harassment of witnesses or underhand dealings could seriously compromise my client and adversely affect the outcome of his trial. My client has been charged with a heinous crime, and he will be tried under the criminal justice system. I am a qualified solicitor working within that system. I cannot pretend that I am happy that Mr Wallace has seen fit to employ your services.' There was a ring of malice in his tone of voice. I was rubbish. 'My experience is that unqualified amateurs, albeit well-intentioned, can rarely contribute anything of value and all too often do harm where they would wish to do good.'

My cheeks were burning. I breathed in and out very slowly and studied a mole to the left of his nose. He passed me the piece of paper.

'Goodbye, Mr Pitt.'

'Ms Kilkenny.'

My restraint broke as I barrelled along Deansgate towards the station. 'Arrogant bastard. Prat. Who the hell does he think he is?' I muttered and cursed. People gave me a wide berth. I didn't care. It had taken all my control not to rise to Pitt's bait, not to argue the toss or try and needle him as he had me, but I couldn't jeopardize the job like that. He had the power to withhold the information I wanted. Oh, probably not for ever. I could have got Luke to request it in writing, or even found the addresses a more convoluted way, but time was flying by and my pride had to be sacrificed to the urgency of the job in hand.

My mobile rang when I was halfway across town heading for the buses at Piccadilly Gardens. It was Debbie Gosforth. The stalker was back.

There's a black Hackney-cab stand near the statue of Queen Victoria. I asked the driver to drop me at the bottom of Chorlton Green. From there I could walk along Debbie's street. I needed a way to loiter without looking suspicious. Nothing occurred during the journey. The driver chatted about the Euro '96 results. I was aware that the Championship was on and that Manchester was full of European football supporters, but I hadn't joined Ray in watching any of the matches on the television.

The sun was hot but there was a light breeze, just enough to stir the branches of the trees on the main road. There was no one about on Debbie's street and I felt conspicuous as I walked along.

He was there. My heart kicked in my chest. I stopped

to tie my lace before I got too close. Debbie's description had been accurate. Slim, dark hair, probably late thirties or early forties. In his suit he looked like a displaced bank clerk or estate agent. Presumably he didn't have a regular job if he turned up at all times of the day and night.

I straightened up and carried on purposefully, past Debbie's house to the crossroads at the corner. I looked up and down the side street for some inspiration, something to do, somewhere to wait where I could keep an eye on him without drawing too much attention to myself. Nothing. No phone box, no bench, no shops. Certainly no convenient vantage point. I turned left and walked along until I was sure he couldn't see me then I rang Debbie's number.

'Debbie, it's Sal. I'm round the corner on Royal Avenue. I've just walked past him. There's nowhere here I can wait, I'm not in the car. Can I get to yours the back way?'

'Yes, down the alley.'

'What's your gate like?'

'Green – look for the climbing frame.'

'OK, see you in a minute.'

It was easy to find. The small back yard held the climbing frame on a patch of parched grass and a wheelie bin. Debbie was on the back doorstep.

'Thanks.' She looked completely washed out. 'You can watch him from the front room,' she said.

'Are you all right?'

She didn't speak for a minute. 'Not really, no. Last night, he kept ringing. Every few minutes, on and on. I'm so tired. I left the phone off the hook in the end. I hate doing that. If my Mum needed anything . . .' She was close to tears.

'We can report it,' I said, 'was it a payphone? Have you tried 1471?'

She shook her head.

'Can I? Has anyone rung you since?'

'No.'

52

I dialled the call-back facility. The recorded voice told me that a call had been made at 3.43 and that the caller had chosen to withhold their number. Great.

'Have you got a phone book . . . the ordinary one?' She went to the cupboard where she'd kept the letters and returned with the one book. I showed her the section in the front where the number was given for malicious calls.

'Ring them,' I said, 'explain that the calls are from someone who is following you and harassing you, and that you've already been to see a solicitor. I'm sure they'll be able to help. They can monitor your calls or they might give you a new number. You could go ex-directory.'

'Yes.' She didn't seem exactly galvanized by my suggestion. For a moment I wanted to shake her, encourage her to show some of her anger instead of this depressed resignation, then reminded myself that she'd hardly slept and that it probably felt to her as though things were just getting worse in spite of outside involvement.

'We will sort it out, you know,' I said, 'though it might feel hopeless at the moment. What did he say on the phone?'

'At first he was just going on like the letters. I kept hanging up. He got angry. He said . . .' she swallowed and her hand pulled at the gold chain around her neck. 'He said I was betraying him and I'd pay for it.' Her voice squeaked and she turned away. 'Would you like some tea?' She needed to cry but she didn't want company.

'Yes, please. No sugar.'

I sat on the arm of the chair in the front room. From there I'd a clear view of the man opposite. I carry a small camera with a zoom lens whenever can. One of the tools of the trade. I thanked my lucky stars that I hadn't taken it out of my bag when I'd gone to town. I set it up, moved the vase of dried flowers from the windowsill, which left a clear section beneath the scalloped nets, and focused on the stalker. He was almost immobile, only shifting occasionally from foot to foot. He stood like someone at a formal service, a funeral or a wedding, arms hanging down in front, hands together, fingers laced. He waited slightly inside the alleyway so he was only easily visible from across the road. I snapped half a dozen shots of the man. Had any of Debbie's neighbours noticed him yet?

She came back with my tea. Her hand was shaking as I took it from her. I was parched; I blew the steam to cool it down enough to drink.

'Is there any news about work?'

'No, it's complete chaos. Jack, he's the owner, he's been into the Town Hall and got his pass but he couldn't even get in to see the place till yesterday. He says it's a right mess, the stock's ruined. There's loads of water damage with the sprinklers going off. The insurance company won't give him a straight answer yet. I'm laid off, officially. Unofficially . . .'

'He's moving,' and I hadn't even had my tea. Talk about inconsiderate. I jumped to my feet. The man had set off towards the main road. 'I'll ring you later. Watch and tell me when he's out of sight, I don't want him to see me coming out of here.'

She moved up to the net curtains as I went through to the front door.

'Debbie,' I called, 'is the door locked?'

'Oh, yes.'

She ran through with the keys.

'You're best with just the Yale on when you're in,' I said, 'and the chain. If there was a fire . . .'

She looked at me, her mouth tight. 'I feel safer.'

And if anyone broke in the back way she'd be trapped.

She ran back into the lounge. 'He's gone.'

I opened the door and walked briskly out to the pavement. My stomach was tightening in excitement. He was up ahead. Now I'd got him. Trail him home, get the address, a word with the neighbours or the local shop and

54

I'd have his identity. Get it to Rebecca along with details of the harassment and she could start the proceedings. In the distance he'd reached one of the side roads to the left. He turned into it. I was puzzled. Why wasn't he heading for the bus stops on the main road at the end? Did he live locally, perhaps? I ran to the corner, slowing as I reached it. There he was, fifty yards down on the left. He'd stopped. Hands in his pockets.

I watched him turn, stoop, open the car door, get in and drive away. A blue car, a Ford – a Fiesta, perhaps. I got part of the number plate. Then he was gone.

Shit, shit, shit.

CHAPTER EIGHT

No tantrums, no whining, no bickering. Just good food and good company. The height of luxury. Diane was a foodie, she loved to eat and had the figure to prove it. Big. And was happy to flaunt it. She dressed adventurously and spent a small fortune on haircuts; her current one was a blue-black urchin look.

She'd set out the table in the middle of her studio-cum-living room. The place was chaotic; canvases, paints and inks, screens, sewing machine, headless dressmaker's dummy, PC, telly in the corner, couch. She lived and worked downstairs and slept upstairs. After twelve years the neighbours had got used to the harmless eccentric in their midst. A couple of them had even commissioned small pieces from her for birthday presents.

'Sit down,' she said after I'd handed her the bottle I'd brought. 'It's ready.'

We exchanged news and gossip as we demolished a plate of cracked olives, tomato and basil salad and hunks of sesame seed bread. But she saved up the best titbit till we'd wiped the plates clean.

'I've had a date,' she announced.

'When? Why didn't you tell me? Who?' I was all indignation.

'A soulmate.'

'What?'

'In the *Guardian*, lonely hearts?' she smiled.

'What was he like?'

Her smile faded. ' 'Orrible,' she sighed, 'we went for a pizza in town, then to the pictures.' She made it sound like a trip to the dentist. 'He's a teacher, recently divorced, three kids. Oh Sal, it was awful. He was obviously depressed and looking for someone to save him.'

'Couldn't you tell, from the ad?'

'No, or I wouldn't have gone. It was one of these where you ring them up, listen to a message. He sounded quite perky.'

'Perky?' I pulled a face.

'Well, you know, lively. I left a message and I made it clear, I really did, that I wasn't looking for anything deep and meaningful, right? Just a bit of pleasant company, no big deal, nothing serious. OK. He rings me up, makes a date. I get there. He wants another wife, virtually said so, probably wants another three kids and all.' She shuddered. Diane had made her mind up in her early twenties that motherhood was not for her. She's never wavered from that belief. 'In fact,' she scooped the plates up, 'I reckon he wants the wife he had before, the kids, the lot. Oh, it was miserable.' She took the plates through to the kitchen.

I filled our glasses. 'Will you try again?'

'I expect so.' She came and sat down again, and took a drink. 'You ought to have a go.'

'Oh no!' I was horrified. 'I couldn't.'

'Why not?'

'It's so . . .'

'Obvious? Well, how else are you ever going to meet anyone?'

'Who says I want to meet anyone?' I retorted. 'I might be perfectly happy as I am.'

'Huh!' She snorted. 'Are you?'

'Yes, most of the time.' I swigged my wine. 'There's a lot to be said for being single,' I went on. 'I don't have to negotiate with someone all the time, I can be as selfish, independent . . .'

She burst out laughing.

'What?'

'Sal, you live with two children, a man, a lodger and a dog. You can't move a muscle without checking out childcare or whether you're out of milk. You're hardly the embodiment of a free spirit.'

'You know what I mean.'

'Whereas I actually am a free spirit. I don't even have a budgie and I could do with a bit of passion.' She fetched a newspaper from the corner. 'Here, look at these.' Some of the ads had been circled.

'How do you pick them?'

'Knock out all the g.s.o.h.'s – good sense of humour. I reckon it's a code, means they're total prats who like practical jokes and toilet humour. And I knock out all the super sporty ones and the very rich ones and the attractive twenty-somethings.'

'Why?'

'I want a man,' she swivelled her shoulders, 'not a boy. Read what's left.'

While she sorted the meal out I read out the five remaining entries. We got giggly reading between the lines. They all sounded inoffensive; one or two were more interesting. One was a keen gardener.

'You see,' she pointed at me with the serving spoon, 'he might be able to help you with your pruning.'

'Ha ha.'

She brought in the main course. A glistening Spanoka-pita, spinach, curd cheese and nuts in a delicate filo pastry, baby new potatoes and a crunchy sprouted salad. Our conversation lulled while we piled up our plates.

'It's wonderful,' I told her.

'You busy?'

'Yes, all of a sudden.' I told her about my week, the

gruesome discovery at Mr Kearsal's, the press follow-up. The bomb.

'I felt it here,' she said, 'the blast. I felt the windows move.' She shook her head. 'I hated that building, but . . .'

We were quiet for a moment, the atmosphere in the room suddenly charged with emotion.

I talked to her about the two cases I now had. I know I can trust her not to gossip to anyone else about my work.

Some more wine, some apricot fool and some fierce coffee, and it was time for home. I cycled back slowly. It was cloudy, no stars to gaze at, but the gardens were full of night scents; sweet stocks, the tang of honeysuckle, heady tobacco plants. Cats were out and about, darting across the roads, creeping under hedges. I passed a dead hedgehog. There wasn't much traffic on the side roads and I could drop my guard and relish the sensation of the air on my face and the tingle in my leg muscles as I built up speed.

CHAPTER NINE

The two witnesses who had allegedly seen Luke Wallace stab Ahktar Khan were Sonia and Rashid Siddiq. They lived in Whitefield not far from Prestwich in one of those new townhouse developments. Tall, thin houses with integral garages clustered round a central courtyard. Two or three-bedroomed properties, twenty of them, each with a tiny spit of land smaller than the old back yards of the red-brick Manchester terraces. There were plenty of olde-worlde features to distract from the economies of scale; mullioned windows, carriage lamps, wood stained fencing, studded doors. But this was the end of the twentieth century, and each house sported a burglar alarm and a satellite dish.

There was a car parked in the driveway of number 18 – a smart white Saab. The lion's-mouth door-knocker made a frightful din that echoed round the courtyard. Most houses looked deserted, their owners out at work. A woman at the far end was loading small children into a hatchback.

I was about to knock again when the door opened, just a few inches.

'Mrs Siddiq?'

She was young. Her eyes narrowed in suspicion. 'Yes?'

'My name is Sal Kilkenny, this is my card.' I passed it to her. 'I'm a private investigator.'

She examined the card carefully as if it could reveal the nature of my enquiry.

'I'd like to ask you a few questions.'

'What's all this about?' she snapped.

'You witnessed an attack on Ahktar Khan.'

She blanched. What else did she think a PI would be calling on her for?

'I've already told everyone about that. The police, the lawyers.' She made a move to shut the door.

'Please,' I said, 'I need to know what you saw. I'll try not to take up too much of your time.'

She hesitated. I took the chance to keep talking.

'I'm sorry to ask you to go over it all again; it must have been very traumatic, but your evidence is crucial. And whatever happened, my client has the right to a fair hearing. It's my job to go over all the evidence and talk to all the witnesses.'

I wasn't getting anywhere. She tried to close the door again.

'Has someone been threatening you?' I asked gently. 'If anyone's put you under any pressure not to talk I'd be expected to notify the police.' Not strictly true but it certainly rang bells for Sonia Siddiq.

She swallowed and stood back. 'No, nobody has. It's just so horrible, like you say.'

The lounge was at the end of the small hallway. It was dominated by several intricately designed rugs on both the walls and the floor, and by a large white leather couch and matching armchairs. An old-fashioned elaborately carved sideboard was covered in silver-framed photographs, candelabra and statuettes. One corner of the room held the consumer durables; CD midi system, video and television.

The armchair crackled under me. Mrs Siddiq perched on one end of the sofa. She was slightly built, which added to the impression of youth. She wore shalwar kameez in a soft caramel colour with silver threads around the borders. Her hair was shoulder length; silver globe earrings hung bright in her ears.

I asked her to tell me everything she could remember from New Year's Eve.

61

'We were going home, we'd been in the club. We'd parked in a side street round the back.'

'Who was driving?'

I wanted to establish whether the Siddiqs had been sober that evening, how reliable they were as witnesses.

She looked puzzled. 'I was.' But she didn't sound very certain.

'Had you had anything to drink?'

'I don't drink.'

I nodded.

'As we came round the corner, there were these two lads arguing and one of them, he had a knife.'

'You could see the knife?'

'Yes, it was quite big. And the other one kicks out and the lad with the knife screams like he's hurt, and then he swings the knife up and they both fall over.' She was disturbed by her recitation; her fingers knotting round themselves, her words breathy.

'What happened then?'

'Excuse me.' She rooted in the sideboard and found what she was looking for, a book of matches, a cigarette.

'Rashid doesn't like me to smoke,' she shrugged her shoulders, 'although he smokes all the time.' She dragged on the cigarette as if she'd suck all the tobacco out, pulling the smoke in deep and holding her breath before releasing it through her nose. I could recall from my own distant past the gloriously dizzying effect of the nicotine as it charged round the system, the buzzing at the back of the neck, the satisfying hit on the throat.

She took another drag.

'We went home.' She spoke with smoke in her lungs.

I stared at her.

She exhaled. 'It's shameful, I know. We were . . . I was frightened to get involved. They were drunk, there was a knife, anything could have happened.'

Anything did. Ahktar died.

'You didn't ring for an ambulance?'

'I wish I could say different.' She lowered her voice, 'Rashid said someone else would get an ambulance or call the police. I think maybe the shock . . .' She broke off. There could be no justification.

'But you did contact the police?'

'The next day, the day after. We heard that he'd died and—'

'Ahktar?'

'Yes.'

'Did you know him?' I asked.

She stared at me. 'No, no.' She shook her head emphatically. 'I didn't know him. We never knew him.'

'I thought perhaps from the club . . . ?'

'No, I'm sure. Neither of us knew him.' She was rattled. Understandable. Bad enough to walk on by while someone bleeds to death; even worse to think you might have known them.

'How did you hear?' I asked her.

'Sorry?'

'About the death. There weren't any papers on New Year's Day.'

She paused. 'The radio, there was something on the radio.'

'OK. So you went to the police on New Year's Day?'

'Yes.' She took another long drag on the cigarette. 'We told them what we'd seen and they arranged an identity parade.'

'And you both picked the same suspect?'

'Yes.'

'Had you seen him before?'

'No, only that night.'

They'd been very reluctant to get involved. So reluctant that they didn't even phone for an ambulance or alert the security staff at the club, but the next day they were contacting the police like model citizens. 'What made you go to the police?'

She shrugged. 'We'd seen what happened. We felt obliged . . .' She tasted filter and grimaced, ground out the cigarette in a large glass ashtray. 'Is there anything else?' She tried to be dismissive but there was no conviction behind the phrase.

'Just a few points,' I said. 'What time did you get to the club?'

'About ten o'clock.'

Luke and friends had gone early knowing it would sell out.

'Did you meet friends?'

She looked perplexed. 'No.'

'Just the two of you?' I sounded surprised.

'Yes, just the two of us.'

'And you didn't bump into anybody by chance, no acquaintances, friends?'

'No,' she insisted. 'It's not somewhere we usually go; we don't know those people.'

'So why were you there?'

'I don't see what this has to do with anything.' She stood up 'I've helped you all I can, now please . . .'

'You didn't drink. Did Rashid?'

'A little.' She shook her head impatiently.

'I'd like to see Mr Siddiq,' I said, 'when's a good time to catch him?'

'Why?' She looked appalled.

'To hear his version of events.'

'It's the same as mine,' she said urgently.

'There are always differences in what people notice, what they remember.'

Unless they're rehearsing a story.

'We identified the same man,' she said, 'we both saw what he did. The police believe us. You'd better go.'

'OK. Thank you for your time. When can I call on Mr Siddiq?'

'I don't know, he's very busy.'

'Where does he work? I could call in, perhaps?'

She hesitated. She was behaving like a suspect, not a witness. What the hell was going on? 'Or I could come back here one evening?' She paled.

'Is there something wrong?'

'No. No,' she blinked. 'He's just . . . very busy.'

I smiled. 'It shouldn't take too long. Where does he work?'

I could see her trying to decide whether she should tell me. 'Are you sure there's nothing wrong?' I pushed her.

'No.' She gave a little laugh, brittle. 'Just he's busy, you know.' She gave up. 'The Asian Cash and Carry on Upper Brook Street.'

'Thank you.'

She was quiet as she saw me out. Muttered goodbye at the door. If the prosecution were going to use her as a witness she'd need plenty of coaching. I'd found her responses puzzling, veering from guilt to indignation.

Why was she so anxious about my intention to interview her husband? What was she so frightened of? Him? What he might say? What also intrigued me was that some of the seemingly innocuous questions about the evening itself had riled her as much as those about the murder and their inhumane response. Questions about why they were there, who'd driven and who they'd met. Now why would those upset her so?

It would be interesting to see if Rashid Siddiq was as defensive as his wife had been.

CHAPTER TEN

I'd no doubt that Mrs Siddiq would alert her husband to my interest, and the longer I left it the more time they would have to confer. I was ninety-nine per cent sure that she'd been lying to me, but I still ran through other explanations for her manner; guilt at not reporting the attack, previous unpleasant dealings with the police, or maybe emotional problems that had nothing to do with the case itself. Had I just caught her on a bad day? She'd certainly been mercurial, her reactions running the gamut from hostility to anxiety.

The Cash and Carry was built with security in mind rather than any aesthetic consideration. It was a large metal cube in a compound of wire netting topped with savage barbed wire. Stanchions sported cameras and lights. The car park was almost full; traders were busy loading crates and drums into vans and cars.

I went in through the automatic doors and surveyed the warehouse. The huge space was divided into aisles by metal shelving which stretched up towards the ceiling. The place was illuminated by harsh strip lighting which gave everything a washed-out look. It smelt of damp cardboard. A sign pointed the way to an empty enquiries desk placed in front of two long prefabricated sections with frosted windows and doors which I took to be the offices.

I rang the bell on the counter and after a few moments a young man in a brown suit appeared from the nearest door. I asked for Mr Siddiq and passed over my card. He went back into the prefab and I watched his shadow disappear from view. When he returned he told me that Mr Siddiq was busy in a meeting. This I translated as: 'Mr Siddiq is in and he's told me to get rid of you.'

'Will he be long?' I asked.

The guy's face darkened with embarrassment. 'He didn't say.'

'I could wait?'

'No,' he coughed. 'It'd be better if you made an appointment.'

'Can I do that now?'

He looked even more uncomfortable. 'You need to see Mr Siddiq? Try ringing.'

'OK,' I said, 'can you tell me his official title?' Apparently not, from the blank look on his face. 'What does he do here?' I prompted.

'He's one of the bosses. He sorts out the deliveries, transfers, transport, that sort of thing . . . and he's in charge of security.' He paused, trying to remember if he'd missed anything.

'And who owns the business.'

He shrugged.

'Well, who's in charge?'

'Mr Khan.'

'Thanks.'

It took ten minutes for a man I presumed to be Rashid Siddiq to leave the building and climb into one of the cars parked in reserved bays off to my left. I angled my rear mirror until I could see him in it.

I'd found sunglasses and a baseball hat in the car and put these on just in case Siddiq had taken a peek at me while I'd grilled his employee. I pretended to study an A–Z, head down while my eyes locked onto the mirror.

I watched as he punched numbers into a mobile phone. I'd a fair idea who he was ringing. From the look on his face and the way he hit the steering wheel with his clenched fist I don't think he liked what he heard.

Mr Siddiq finished his call then started his car up and reversed out of his space. I followed, allowing a couple of cars to come between us. He skirted town along Great Ancoats Street, past the old Daily Express building with its glass and Art Deco façade. I was old enough to remember seeing the papers rolling off the presses there – like something out of Citizen Kane. Down past the CIS building, famed for its height rather than its beauty, and over the bridge to the bottom of Cheetham Hill Road. He stopped part-way up in a car park adjacent to a large clothing wholesalers.

It was a brilliant building, or had been in its heyday, like a Georgian country house standing foursquare, with pillars around the front entrance and broad steps down to the street. There were huge windows on both storeys, a real liability for this inner city spot. They were covered with sheets of metal, grilles and wood, no two alike and daubed with graffiti.

There was a petrol station conveniently placed opposite. I'd time to check my tyres and top up with petrol. I bought a plain Bounty bar and a small bottle of water with a hint of lemon. Well, I meant to get a hint of lemon but I ended up with a peach one which tasted like liquid potpourri.

Huge signs on the front of the building told me it was *J.K. Imports* and proclaimed *International Labels*, *All Discount Stock*, *Best Deals in Town* and *Trade Only*. I could hardly go in and browse then. And he showed no sign of coming out. I concluded that Mr Siddiq was probably now back doing business having spoken to his wife. Luke Wallace had mentioned that the Khan brothers had a place up Cheetham Hill. This was probably it. J.K. – Janghir Khan. I could sit and stare at the building all afternoon and learn nothing.

Time to go.

I dropped off the film that had the pictures of the stalker for same-day processing on my way to the office.

From there I rang Ahktar's father, Dr L. P. L. Khan. 'Dr Khan?'

'Yes, speaking.'

I told him who I was, what I wanted. I asked to see him. There was a long pause.

'I will be at home tomorrow between half past ten and eleven o'clock,' he said.

'And Mrs Khan?'

'Mrs Khan is visiting her family in Pakistan. She will be away until September.'

'Right. I'll see you at half past ten then. Thank you.'

The phone rang as soon as I put it down. I hate that. It startled me and sent shivers of shock up my arms. 'Hello?'

'Sal, Rebecca Henderson here. Debbie Gosforth tells me there have been some problems with the surveillance.'

Oh, great. 'Just one,' I defended myself. 'We assumed he had no car so I was all prepared to tail him on foot, but he was using a car. Parked round the corner.'

'You got the number?'

'Only partial.'

Silence. If I was paying a solicitor, there'd be endless delays and hiccups to put up with, but turn the tables and I'm expected to produce instant results.

'Listen, I know we said we didn't need twenty-four hour cover,' Rebecca resumed finally, 'but if you don't feel you can give this one the time . . .'

'Hang on,' I interrupted, 'am I missing something here? I've been over there twice as soon as she's called. The first time he'd already gone when I arrived and the second time he's driving, which we knew nothing about. I've also advised her to get on to the phone company and fix up a new number or go ex-directory. She knows she can ring me anytime, as soon as he shows.'

'Have you met her brother?'

'Eh? No. Why?'

'I've had him on the phone ranting about how little we're doing. He says Debbie is scared to leave the house, that the threats are escalating and that she thinks you're only going through the motions, can't wait to get away.'

'That's not true,' I objected. I thought back to my visits. 'The first time she called me it was getting dark. I came out, no problem. I even offered to see her at the house when we knew the stalker had gone but she put me off, she was worried it would wake one of the children.' I was getting riled. 'The second time when he drove off I did go back to the house to tell her. I offered to come in for a few minutes, asked if there was anything else she wanted me to do.'

'Hmmm.' Rebecca gave a non-committal grunt. 'And you told her she was being paranoid locking the doors when she was in the house on her own?'

'Oh, for heaven's sake!' I exploded. 'I don't know where all this has come from, but I'm doing the job you hired me to do. Now if she's got problems with me or wants someone else then fine, I'll send you an invoice but there is no question of shoddy work. Maybe she needs a bodyguard as well.'

'I think the brother's limbering up for that. I'm sorry, Sal, it sounds as if there's some manipulation going on here. I thought it didn't sound like you but I had to ask. Stay with it for now,' she decided, 'if you're prepared to, and I'll get in touch with her and explain exactly what we are hiring you to do. I'll put it in writing too so there's no mistake. I'll point out the other things she can do like the ex-directory stuff. Let me know if you meet any resistance.'

I agreed to carry on but came off the phone smarting, not least because I'd failed to pick up on any hint of hostility from Debbie Gosforth. Her complaints were an unexpected slap in the face. I wished that she had given me some indication of her concerns about my work. I suffer from an acute sense of justice and fair play, and I was outraged that I'd not had a chance to answer Debbie's accusations before she'd run off to Rebecca with them, or to this brother. I knew I'd have to put things in perspective before I saw her again, but meanwhile I needed to work off some of the useless indignation that was fizzing round my bloodstream.

I called home for my swimsuit and towel and cycled down to the baths in Withington. After twenty lengths I'd mentally barracked Debbie Gosforth, and Rebecca Henderson for listening to her. I'd caught the stalker and been rewarded with huge sums of money and I'd even had a go at Dermott Pitt for his patronizing attitude.

The next twenty lengths I used for more positive fantasies. The sun came in through the glass roof and sparkled and dappled the water. I dreamt of swimming in warm seas, of hot sands underfoot and sudden nightfall. As I showered I decided it was time to make holiday plans, something to look forward to. I wasn't going to get any big rewards no matter what results I got for my clients. There'd be no flights to sun-kissed islands dotted with olive groves for Maddie and me. Camping, more like. Somewhere green and damp like Anglesey or the Lleyn Peninsula. Where dry nights or sunny days would be cause for celebration. Kagool territory. It would do. It would have to.

CHAPTER ELEVEN

With some equilibrium restored I considered how to spend the rest of the afternoon. It would take me too long to get up to North Manchester to interview any of Luke's friends and be back in time for school. I wanted to speak to Debbie but I'd wait until she'd heard from Rebecca. I promised myself I'd pack lots of visits into the following day. I was up in North Manchester seeing Dr Khan then anyway so it would make sense to call on other people on my list. No work till tomorrow, then.

With a grin I decided that there was only one thing to do. The garden.

It was a glorious afternoon and hot enough to change into shorts and T-shirt and slap on some sun cream. I brought in the washing, stiff from the line, and heaped it in a corner for sorting later. I cut the grass with the old roller mower, grunting with the effort and feeling the pull on my stomach muscles. The cuttings went in the compost heap. The sweet peas needed tying in and then I dead-headed the tubs and baskets. I thought again about the beauty and simplicity of the Wallaces' garden. Could I ever do anything like that here? I surveyed the garden. It wouldn't be me really though, would it? And there was more to it than just vision; Mrs Wallace had spent serious money to realize her plans. Even the grass was in a different league, like velvet compared to our rough hessian.

I'd some nasturtiums to plant out but no real room for

them. In the end I decided to get rid of a patch of carnations which were past their best. They'd only managed three blooms the previous year. I loved the sweet milk and clove scent of them but the nasturtiums would give much more colour.

I hate throwing plants away so to soften the blow I took some small stem cuttings from the carnations and potted them up. I knew they were probably not worth the effort but it made me feel better. Earlier I had got the sun-lounger out. Faint hope. It was already schooltime and I hadn't paused. I washed my hands and wandered down the road to collect Maddie and Tom.

Someone in the Khan household had a love of antique furniture. The place looked like something out of a stately home; exquisite inlaid bureaux, corner cupboards and a collection of miniatures and cameos on one wall. The air was fragrant with scent from a vase of lilies. A grandfather clock tick-tocked crisply.

At first Dr Khan was impeccably polite and cold as ice. He offered me tea and when I accepted he asked the young woman I'd seen at the end of the hall to bring it for us.

'My daughter,' he explained, 'she has just finished her Finals.'

'What's she doing?'

He indicated a chair, Regency I think, stripy anyway. 'Optometry.'

Oh. I couldn't think of any useful small talk to make about that; I wasn't even certain what it was, though I knew it had to do with eyes. 'Thank you for seeing me,' I said. 'I've been employed by Mr Wallace, as I explained.'

'Yes.'

'He's convinced of his son's innocence and, as you know, Luke is pleading not guilty.'

'There were witnesses,' he said sharply. The light reflected off his glasses as he straightened in his chair

'Witnesses can make mistakes.'

'That will be for the jury to decide. This is not pleasant for me. If you will come to the point.'

'I'm sorry, I realize it must be difficult having to go over it again. I wouldn't be here if I didn't think it was important. I'm trying to establish exactly what happened. I'll be talking to everybody I can find, if you can tell me the sequence of events that night?'

He cleared his throat softly. Leant forward, arms resting on his thighs, hands clasped between his knees. 'Ahktar and his friends went to the party at the nightclub.'

'You knew he was going?'

'Yes, he was a good boy, he'd been working hard, we were happy to see him have fun too.' He swallowed.

'You knew his friends?'

'Yes, they came here sometimes, they seemed nice enough.'

Our drinks arrived. I'd been half-expecting cups and saucers with all the threat of slops in the saucer and the problem of how to write whilst needing two hands for the crockery, but she'd brought mugs. I took mine thankfully. As she closed the door Dr Khan resumed his story.

'The hospital rang about half past three. They wouldn't tell me anything over the phone, they just said Ahktar had been hurt. I imagined that there had been a car crash. I don't know why, it was my first thought – the taxi home . . .' He took a deep breath, pressed his fist to his mouth, released the air slowly through his knuckles.

'At the hospital I was taken into an anteroom. I knew as soon as I saw the doctor's face. He was so young, he looked as if he had some guilty secret. "I'm very sorry," he said, "Ahktar was admitted here earlier this morning, we tried to revive him but we weren't able to. I'm sorry." I asked then if it had been a car crash. He told me Ahktar had been stabbed – a single blow. They had no other details but the police had been involved; they wanted to see me after I'd—' Dr Khan jumped to his feet; he took a couple of steps away, his back to me, and stood facing the gallery of miniatures on the wall.

I concentrated on my notepad. He removed his glasses and wiped at them with a large white handkerchief. When he began to speak again he continued to face the paintings. 'I must have been over it a hundred times,' his voice was husky, 'but still . . . I had to identify him, my son.' His voice shrank to a whisper, he pressed the handkerchief to his mouth.

I swallowed hard.

'The police asked me lots of questions but I have little recollection of them now. They did ask me about Luke Wallace, and I wondered whether he had been hurt too, but they never answered me.' He turned towards me then, his eyes damp, wide with pain. 'And then I had to come home and tell my wife,' he said bitterly, 'our only son.' He paused. 'He was going to study law, you know. Ironic, isn't it?'

I kept quiet.

'He wanted justice. Well, now I want justice.'

'You wouldn't want the wrong person convicted though?'

He looked at me quizzically.

'Luke Wallace asked me to tell you that he didn't hurt Ahktar. He's devastated by his death.'

'The court will decide.'

'But you seem to have made up your mind already.'

'People saw him do it. The police have statements. There was an argument. What am I supposed to think?' He raised his voice, anger flashing in his eyes.

'Luke had no reason—' I began.

'Ahktar's death is senseless!' he shouted. 'There can be no reason, it is beyond reason.' Silence stretched in the wake of his outburst. 'We may never discover why Ahktar was killed,' he said, 'but I will learn how. The facts become terribly important, I've noticed this in my own practice, with accidental death, with suicides. The details, the time, the place, the sequence; it helps to know. Please, Miss Kilkenny, I have nothing else to say.'

I put down my mug and got to my feet. 'You said something about an argument?'

He sighed. Pinched at the bridge of his nose. 'Zeb, Rangzeb, Ahktar's cousin was there that night. He saw them arguing. It came out at the committal hearing.'

'What was it about?'

'I've no idea. Speak to Zeb.'

CHAPTER TWELVE

There are many reasons why people agree to talk to private investigators. A lot of them simply like the attention; they like to be listened to, to have a new audience for their account. It may be that there aren't very many people they can tell, or those they have told don't want to hear it again. Someone like me comes along who is passionately interested in what they have to say, and they feel validated, important, responsible again.

If the circumstances were upsetting, the visit from an investigator can be a chance to get it all out in the open once more. Other people don't realize they have a choice, and some would consider it ill-mannered to refuse.

In Zeb's case, as I later discovered, he had good reasons for wanting to appear co-operative, since he had something to hide. Like the Siddiqs. Trouble was, he couldn't quite carry it off. His personality got the better of him.

I'd rung the bell twice and was about to give up when the intercom crackled. I put my face close to the speaker.

'Sal Kilkenny. I'd like to speak to Zeb Khan.'

The buzzer sounded and I pushed the door and went into the lobby. I was glad to find him awake – if he'd been playing the tables the previous night he might not have got to bed till after sunrise.

The flats, a block of eight, were set in landscaped gardens with parking at the back. Each flat occupied a corner position with picture windows on either side.

Zeb's flat was on the first floor. He opened his door but didn't invite me in, 'What is it?'

'I'm investigating Ahktar's death,' I said, 'I'd like to talk to you.'

His expression shifted but I couldn't read it. Embarrassment? Discomfort? Ahktar had been his cousin, after all.

He stood back and let me in. The living room smelt of stale cigarette smoke and fresh coffee. The space was bland; neutral shades for everything, no pictures or ornaments, no plants. Comfortable, clean but impersonal. Zeb obviously didn't bother making statements with his interior decoration but his clothes were another matter. He wore the latest designer styles, an Armani T shirt and Calvin Klein jeans. It was easy to tell – the labels were on the outside, writ large.

He had the sort of sulky good looks that fill the magazines and are found in boys' pop groups; slightly pouting lips, dark eyes, squared-off jaw and matching cheekbones, tousled hair and perfect skin.

We sat down and I explained why I was involved in the investigation and apologized for asking him to go over it all again.

'Were you close to Ahktar?' I began. 'I know you were cousins. Did you spend much time together?'

He shook his head. 'I was working and he was studying for his exams, to get into university.'

'He wanted to do law.'

'Yeah, we're not all shopkeepers, you know.'

And we're not all bigots. His belligerence shocked me.

'You're wasting your time,' he said bluntly.

'What makes you say that?'

' 'Cos they know who did it – Luke Wallace. They've got witnesses and everything.'

'Do you know the Siddiqs?'

'What?' He was thrown by the question. I repeated it.

'No – well, I know who they are, 'cos of all this, but why?'

78

'Rashid Siddiq works for your brother, at the Cash and Carry. You don't know him?'

'No. It's a big company, I can't keep track of all the people there.' There was an aggressive edge to his manner that kept me alert, ready to leave if I needed to.

I tried again, 'What do you think happened?'

'Wallace stabbed him. He was out of his head – it happens, doesn't it? Some people take something and it sends them crazy. He probably didn't know what he was doing. They reckon he can't remember any of it.'

'So you don't think Luke intended to hurt him, he just lost control?'

'No,' he contradicted himself, 'they'd been arguing, earlier on.'

I waited for him to continue but he didn't.

'You saw them?' I prompted.

'They were just arguing, mouthing off at each other,' he said irritably.

'Do you know what it was about?'

'No, I couldn't hear.'

'When was this?'

'I don't know.'

'What time did you get there?'

' 'Bout eight.'

'So when you saw them arguing was it soon after that?'

'No.'

'Before Emma left?'

He frowned, sat forward in his seat then back again. He wasn't sure. I was perplexed by his reactions but then I thought of an explanation.

'You'd taken drugs as well?' I said. 'It makes it harder to remember exactly when everything happened?'

'No. Yeah.' He ran a hand through his hair. 'I'd had a tab but I remember, I saw them. Going at it they were, screaming at each other. Emma had gone, yeah, it was later, after she'd gone.' He nodded to himself as if he'd found the correct answer.

'Why did she leave?'

'What's that got to do with it?' he bristled. 'That's got fuck all to do with it.'

I shrugged. 'OK. You were seen having a go at Joey D. What was that about?'

'I've had enough of this,' he said in disgust. 'I don't have to listen to this. We're going to win this one. That guy's going to pay for Ahktar. You can ask all the questions you like, it won't change anything. I know what I saw and the police have got all the evidence they need.'

'After the argument,' I persisted, 'did you see Ahktar later?'

'No.' He was almost vehement. 'It was packed. They were still dancing. I went to chill out.'

'You didn't see him again?'

He shook his head impatiently.

'Can you think of anyone else who might have had a grudge against Ahktar?'

'Look, do you think they'd prosecute if it wasn't watertight, eh? Dead Paki. It wouldn't get anywhere near a court if it wasn't a fucking certainty that Wallace did it. You come round here trying to pick holes in it all, find a way for him to wriggle out. Well, forget it – right? Fucking forget it.'

It was time to go.

I stood up. 'Does Emma still live in Whalley Range?'

He shrugged.

'Don't you see her any . . . ?'

His look stopped me mid-sentence. It was murderous.

I nodded once then turned and walked briskly to the door. My heart squeezed. I could feel his eyes on my back, sense the anger thick as fog.

I'd been here before, other men, other rooms, that same unsteadying realization of danger. A hair's breadth from violence.

I thought of Debbie Gosforth. Tidying up, keeping things in order while the threat of violence hovered over her shoulder.

I forced myself not to bolt. At the door I turned and said a short goodbye.

A thin film of sweat slicked my body from head to toe. I sat in the car with the window down and breathed slowly till my heart let go and my skin became cold and clammy.

Mrs Deason, Joey D's grandmother, welcomed me into her home like a long-lost relative. She was desperate to talk, I think. To anyone who would listen. And Joey was her favourite topic.

The house looked like some colonial villa, with a fancy tiled roof, shuttered windows and palm trees mixing with the conifers and rhododendrons in the driveway.

Inside, the place was cluttered with heavy antique furniture, festooned with carvings, ornaments and pictures from China. There was a smell of snuff and polish and apples.

Joey wasn't there; he'd run away from home, he'd done it before. She showed me photographs of him, school portraits and holiday snaps, some in the hall, others in the lounge. Her eyes shining with pride as she spoke of him. 'He is such a charmer, the sweetest disposition. And when you think what he's been through. But he hasn't a mean streak in him.'

Yes, I could ask her some questions. She established that I hadn't had lunch and then prepared what she called a summer brunch for us to eat on the terrace.

There was tons of it; prawn salad, three types of bread, potato and egg salad, coleslaw, mini-quiches, chicken drumsticks and cold cuts of meat. I'd explained I didn't eat meat.

'Oh, don't worry, dear, I will.' And she did. Thin as a rake, with wispy hair and hands riddled with arthritis, she had munched her way through most of the spread with great relish.

'I felt I had so much to make up for, with Joey. You see, I didn't realize about John, my son – Joey's father, for years. There'd been some trouble in his teens but I'd no idea he was an alcoholic. I blamed the recession when the business sank, but then it happened again. It was Patsy who told me, his wife, she wrote to me. I was up in Cumbria. I didn't believe her. He was drinking it all away. He owed money everywhere, he'd taken money from friends, business associates, he'd remortgaged the house without even telling her.' She took a swig from her glass of lemonade and smacked her lips with pleasure.

I had another mouthful of salad and caught the scent of old roses on the breeze.

'He was never violent, just . . . completely unreliable, untrustworthy. Patsy left; she was very young, she went back to America. She was going to send for Joey, but . . . she was very young,' Mrs Deason said again, looking into the distance. When she caught herself at it she snapped back to attention. 'Joey stayed here, while his father was in and out of clinics and under various specialists. He had cirrhosis. As time went on, Patsy met someone else – and reading between the lines, I don't think her new man would have made Joey very welcome. I'd moved in by then. Joey was six. It seemed best to just carry on. Nothing worked for long. John couldn't stay sober, you see. Then he just gave up. The last I knew of him, he was up in London, living on the streets. He knows he can always come here but I don't think he could bear it – for Joey, you know. And it sounds – awful but I pray he'll stay where he is. Have you any experience of alcoholism?'

I shook my head.

'It destroys everybody, not just the drinker, everything,' she sighed. 'They talk about drugs, but . . . anyway, it didn't take me long to see how deeply Joey had been affected. Crying out for attention but a good boy, helpful, eager to please, desperate for praise. You know, he used to look after John when he was drunk – clean him up, put him to bed. What does that do to a small child? Trying to save his father, the same man who would steal his Christmas presents and sell them.'

She offered me a plate of strawberry tarts. I took one and bit into crisp pastry and firm fruit, releasing the tangy, sweet juice.

'I thought love would be enough, love and a good home, but he began to experiment with drugs. He was only eleven the first time I caught him. He promised it would never happen again,' she smiled ruefully. 'I'd heard that often enough before from John. We never argued, Joey and I,' she said, 'Joey won't argue. He just smiles and tells you what you want to hear and goes on in his own sweet way.'

'And he's run away before?'

'Yes, every so often he just goes. He never tells me where he's been or why he's gone or what's happened to him.'

'How long has he been gone this time?'

'Since New Year's Day.' Just after the murder.

'Did you report him missing?'

'No, he left me a note.'

'Did he say where he was going?'

'No.' She hesitated. 'No, just that he had to go away and not to worry and . . .' she placed the salt and pepper mills neatly together, 'and not to go to the police.'

My stomach turned over. 'Joey carried a knife,' I said quietly.

'I hated that,' she said vehemently. 'I told him about it countless times. It did no good. He told me it kept the bullies away. Joey's small for his age.'

'New Year's Eve, after the party, did you see him?'

'No, I was asleep when he got back.'

'He told you what had happened?'

She delayed her reply while she sipped her lemonade.

I saw Joey. The urchin face smiling from the framed

photographs in the hall. Joey with the knife, Joey arguing with Ahktar, Joey losing control.

'He told me that his friend had been killed. He was shocked, frightened – such a terrible thing.'

'Did the police come?'

'On the Tuesday afternoon they wanted to speak to Joey but he'd gone by then. They asked about his knife.' She paused, then took a steadying breath. 'I reassured them: Joey had his knife here on New Year's Day. That's what we were arguing about, before he left, we had a row. I hated him carrying that thing. I was tired of worrying about that and the drugs, so I took it from his room. Thank God, I was able to show it to them.'

'You've got the knife?'

'Yes.'

'Here?'

She got up from the table and went into the house. I watched bees swaying through the lavender and the breeze lifting the petals on the blowsy roses. But something was wrong. I could sense it in the air, tainting the fragrance of the flowers.

This woman came over as completely convincing. She could lie with an unwavering gaze and the authority of money and age, and everyone would believe her, including the police.

She returned with a soft, chamois-leather bundle and unwound it, slowly exposing the knife, its wooden handle and broad, curving blade. The sun caught the metal which shone hot and blinding for a moment.

I looked at her. She wrapped it up.

'And you've no idea where he is?' Silence. 'Mrs Deason?' The sound of a strimmer starting up a little way away. I tried again. 'Why did Joey run away – the day after the murder?'

'I don't know.' She became flustered. 'I told you we had a row . . .'

84

'You told me before that Joey never argued.'

'Joey wasn't even there. He left before the others, he only heard about the murder later. When we knew the Khan boy had been stabbed I challenged Joey about the foolishness of knives. I demanded that he give me his. He refused. The next chance I had, I took it from his room; he was outraged. Later that day he left.'

'How did you hear about the murder?'

She looked at me, her face blank, panic in her eyes. A simple question but she had no answer. Joey had told her, Joey had been there. I was sure of it.

'Do you know where he is?' I asked now. 'I'm not out to get Joey, my job is to find any evidence that can support my client's claim of innocence.'

'He's not violent, he's never . . . he can't stand the sight of blood.'

Oh, how many times was that phrase used after the event!

'I'm not accusing him,' I said, 'but he was there that night, wasn't he? He came home in a state, next thing, he's run away. He's frightened, he must know something. Please, Mrs Deason: where is he?'

'He was . . .' she was on the brink; she held her hands up cupped close together, a fragile gesture, as though to demonstrate something, but then she let them fall. 'No,' she blurted out, 'no, you're wrong.'

'You've heard from Joey?'

'I don't know where he is,' she insisted, but that wasn't what I'd asked.

'Mrs Deason, whatever Joey knows, whatever he did or didn't do, we have to find out. There's a boy his age sat in a cell awaiting trial for murder. He swears he's innocent. Please, contact him. Ask him if he'll see me, tell him about Luke Wallace. He can't hide for ever. Just ask him, please?'

'I swore that . . . I promised. I have to keep my promise.

His life has been full of broken promises. I'm the only person he can trust. He didn't do anything,' she repeated emphatically.

'I need to hear it from him,' I said, 'that's all I want. He's scared, he's run away, he knows something. Please just ask him if he'll talk to me. He can say no. His friend needs to know the truth. Please ask him.'

I waited, she gave the slightest nod of her head. I gave her my card.

'I won't betray him,' she whispered. 'He's all I have left.' And she looked beyond me to her memories.

CHAPTER THIRTEEN

Perhaps it was that simple. Joey D had stabbed Ahktar and fled. Luke had been found with his friend and assumed to be guilty. Not what the Siddiqs had seen though.

The police had the murder weapon too and Joey's knife was safely at his grandma's.

Whether he was guilty or not, Joey D was scared – so something he'd done or something he knew could get him into trouble. Serious trouble. I groaned with frustration.

I was relieved to find that neither of the other members of the lads' band were in. Now the exams were over, Simon was camping with his brother in Wales and Josh had started a seasonal job at his uncle's hotel in Southport. I was feeling overloaded with all the information I'd got that day.

At this stage in the enquiry I'd not much idea how important it would be to see them, and there were some other people I could interview first in the hope it would become clearer.

I collected Maddie and Tom in the car, as we needed to do a supermarket trip. After an initial squabble about who would push the trolley, they were reasonably co-operative. I smoothed the way by letting them each choose a packet of biscuits and by indulging in some chocolate mousse desserts.

I knew we needed just about everything so I stocked

the trolley high. At the checkout I had a heart-stopping moment when I couldn't find my cheque card. It was in the other half of my purse. Saved.

Ray was glued to the football, England versus Germany at Wembley. But it was a beautiful evening so I settled myself with wine, an Elmore Leonard book that I hadn't read and a plate of olives and crackers. Someone down the road was playing Oasis with the windows wide open, and from the opposite direction I could hear a power saw. As dusk fell the birds quietened and the whining tool stopped. Oasis was followed by M People. They were going to play at Old Trafford on Saturday, supporting Simply Red – a concert to raise money for the Emergency Fund. I laid my book down and watched the stars climb up. A dark shape flew above me, twisting as it went. A bat.

Ray came out. 'We lost, penalty shoot-out.' He seemed devastated.

I'd only a dim grasp of what that meant. 'No goals?' I ventured.

'No. And the poor sod who missed will be blamed for losing the whole match. Southgate, he's called. Yup, that's how he'll be remembered – as the bloke who lost the penalty shoot-out.'

'Wine?' I offered as consolation.

'I've got some lager.' He re-emerged with a can and we sat together for a while as he came down from the match, swapping bits of news about the children and school, and agreeing what still needed to be done for Tom's party.

That night, I dreamt about a knife. I'd lost it in the supermarket. Mrs Deason was asking for it: she wanted it back. Then the police burst in. They knew I was guilty. I reared awake in a state of panic. A dream. Just a dream.

I went quietly downstairs and made myself a cup of elderflower tea with honey. I needed to let the images ebb away. I hate it when aspects of the job invade my night's sleep. It wasn't as if things had got particularly hairy. Not like previous cases when I'd been threatened, assaulted, even shot at. Stupid dream. Be all right if it revealed any answers, but it didn't.

OK, I admitted to myself, it's the knife. Blame the knife. I have a fear of knives. I'd been stabbed once, here in this kitchen, sitting at this very table. Even being shot at hadn't come close to the terror I'd felt as the man held the blade near my neck and whispered threats. Spittle on his lips . . .

I resisted the impulse to jump up and try to run away from the fears. Instead I practised the exercise I'd been taught, playing out the memory, letting it run to the part where he raised his arm, then changing the outcome. I was strong, stronger than him; I grabbed his wrist, wrested the knife from him, broke it in my bare hands, led him away, handed him over to the custodian at the door. I went through it again, and by then I was sleepy enough to return to bed.

I felt a flash of irritation with the dog down the road, who began to bark as soon as I turned off my light. I worked out that it had been eight days since I'd seen Victor Wallace and started to work on the case. All that time for my fears about knives to surface. Not bad, eight days was making progress.

I was nearly off when a taxi came clattering down the road and there was much slamming of doors and jovial farewells. But soon it was quiet again.

And then it was morning.

Something happens to the clock between getting up and the time we have to leave for school. I never actually see it happen, but instead of ticking neatly round minute by minute, it takes great leaps from one figure on the dial to one across the other side. Even more unnerving is the fact that this erratic behaviour is synchronized with all the digital timepieces in the house.

One moment we're making toast, the lunches are packed

89

and there's loads of time, and the next we're terribly late, Maddie's lost her shoes and there's Vimto leaking from Tom's lunchbox.

Returning from school to my office I took ten minutes to drink a cup of coffee, check my mail and messages, come to terms with Maddie's parting words: 'I hate you, pigbum, you always make me late' – and regain a reasonable pulse rate.

My rent was due for the office. I wrote a cheque for the Dobsons and left it upstairs on their kitchen table. It was a modest sum; I certainly couldn't have rented a shoebox for that amount from anyone else.

I rang Rebecca Henderson to check whether she had spoken to Debbie Gosforth as promised. She was out but her secretary Alison remembered typing and posting the letter the previous morning. She'd have got it by now. I'd collected the photos of the stalker and I put them in the folder with my other notes. They were adequate to prove that G had been loitering outside Debbie Gosforth's house on that occasion. Not an offence as such. Neither was stalking, come to that, only if it could be proved there was intent to cause harm. Most stalking cases were prosecuted for other crimes, like malicious damage or assault. You could keep up a campaign of terror against someone for years and the law could do little about it. That was Rebecca Henderson's worry, and Debbie's. Mine was getting the man's name and address as soon as possible.

I put the Gosforth file away and got out the Wallace one. I made notes on my meetings with Mrs Siddiq, Dr Khan, Zeb Khan and Mrs Deason. I have a system of dividing the page into sections. In the first I'd enter facts or alleged facts – what people said they had seen or done or heard, along with times and dates, that sort of thing. In the second section I'd enter anything I wanted to remember about that person's attitude and opinions, their reactions and the impression they had made on me. In the final section I'd jot down all my own hunches and suspicions, questions that went unanswered and doubts I had. I'd allow myself to spin wild scenarios about what the truth might be.

Of course, this was for my eyes only; I'd be appalled if anyone else ever saw it. In a clearcut case there'd be little or nothing in the final section, but as I worked on these reports I was struck by how many queries I had and how muddy everything seemed.

The Siddiqs were witnesses but I got a definite sense that they had some stake in the case. Their reactions hinted at some other involvement; they were not just objective observers. Of course, they did work for a relative of Dr Khan . . . I kept coming back to the fact that they'd left Ahktar to bleed to death. Was their guilt a reason for the extra baggage that they brought to the case? Was that the explanation for all the bad vibes?

Zeb Khan I labelled volatile. He'd reacted aggressively to my visit, even more so when I'd asked about his row with Joey D and when I'd mentioned Emma. He'd been unclear at first about what time in the evening he had seen the two friends arguing. Was that simply the effect of drugs? Had anyone else seen the row? Could he have imagined it, been hallucinating? There was no clue as to what they might have argued about.

Was Zeb a physically violent man? Could he have become embroiled in an argument with his cousin and then, when it ended in tragedy, somehow set Luke up to take the rap?

And if Mr Siddiq was in charge of security at the Cash and Carry, surely Zeb would know him! Even if Zeb was based at the clothing importers up Cheetham Hill Road, he'd still have some passing knowledge of Rashid Siddiq, wouldn't he? I knew for a fact that Siddiq visited J.K. Imports – I'd followed him there.

As for Joey D, he had seen or heard or done something that night that led him to flee, fearing for his safety. He was known to carry a knife similar to the one that killed Ahktar, and he arrived home shocked and scared. I was surprised the police hadn't become more suspicious, given the timing of his flight from home.

Mrs Deason would have been completely plausible. He'd already run away twice that year, she'd said, coming back when the money ran out or things got too heavy. She'd told them about his knife, the argument they'd had about it, the fact that she'd taken it from him. She had shown them it. Proof. So there was no reason to connect the knife used on Ahktar to Joey. The police had plenty of evidence pointing to Luke as it was. Mrs Deason's account fitted the known facts. Their interest in Joey D would have focused on the knife. His weapon could safely be ruled out of the enquiry.

My interest however was more wide-ranging, and I wasn't satisfied, not by a long chalk. I'd uncovered a more disturbing version of Joey D's involvement in the events of that night, but I couldn't go any further without talking to him. There was no point in reporting what I'd learned to the police because I knew Mrs Deason would perjure herself to the hilt to protect her grandson, and she would be totally convincing.

Emma Clegg, Zeb's ex-girlfriend, worked at a nursery in Whalley Range, near Chorlton where Debbie lived. I could call in on Debbie and then carry on for my lunch-time meeting with Emma. I went home and made myself an olive paste, tomato, basil and lettuce submarine sandwich and a flask of chilled pineapple juice. It was a warm day but dull. Hard to tell whether the cloud would clear or open up and soak us. I took my kagool as a precaution. Debbie Gosforth was taken aback to find me on the doorstep. 'He's not here,' she said, bemused.

'I know, I just wanted a word. Can I come in?'

We went into the lounge which was as clean and tidy as ever. 'They're nice.' She'd got a bunch of carnations and gypsophila in a vase by the window.

She nodded, arms folded across herself, not keen on small talk.

'Rebecca Henderson rang me the other day,' I began. 'Apparently, you haven't been very happy with how things are going.'

She looked embarrassed, shook her head, 'No, I . . .'

I gave her a chance to carry on but she couldn't think of what to say.

'Has Rebecca written to you?'

'Yes.'

'And she's explained what I'm expected to do?'

She bobbed her head, blushing.

'Is that all right? Because if you still feel unhappy you can always talk to her about getting someone else in.'

'No, no,' she protested, 'it's fine.'

And that was it. I couldn't make sense of her. She clearly didn't want to be having the discussion at all, and gave me no more idea of what had prompted her complaints.

I asked her to talk to me first if anything else bothered her and we could see if we could sort it out between ourselves.

'Yes,' she said.

In my dreams.

'Have there been any more calls?'

'Last night. He said I'd betrayed him, called me all these names – swearing, awful things.' Her mouth twisted with disgust. 'Names from the Bible, too – Salome, Jezebel, Delilah.' I had a mental picture of Tom Jones crooning, the silhouette of a woman, the knife, the stabbing from the video that had accompanied the song. Tom's throaty Welsh bellow: 'Deli-ilah!'

I concentrated on Debbie. 'Have you rung BT?'

'Yes, well, Ricky did, this morning, after I told him. They said to stay calm and not to talk, put the phone down for a while and then replace the receiver. If it carries on they said they might trace the call, like you said.'

'What about changing your number? Would you rather do that?'

She didn't get a chance to reply as the front doorbell rang. She went to answer it. I heard a man's voice then Debbie's, low and urgent.

'Lost him again, have you?' He came into the room and stood there with his feet apart, legs braced, chin out. He had very short hair, wore stonewashed chinos, a green vest, Doc Martens.

'Ricky,' she said weakly.

'Have you any idea what it's doing to her?' the man blustered. 'He wants putting away, bloody pervert. What's his game, eh? Frightening women? She's scared to look out of the window or answer the phone.' It had to be the brother. Rebecca Henderson had mentioned him. It couldn't be anyone else.

'I know,' I interrupted him, 'and as soon as we find out who he is and where he lives, we can apply for the injunction.'

'Oh, great – and what if he ignores it, what then? He wants locking up now before it goes any further. She's gonna end up in Cheadle Royal if it goes on like this.'

'Ricky, please.'

'Sit down,' he ordered her. She sat. 'She's already on tablets, you know. She should sue him, screw the bastard, what he's done to her nerves. You'll never get him like this,' he pronounced. 'You need to be here all the time. I told her she should get a proper security firm. Lot of them are ex-coppers, they know how to play it. Soon get it sorted.'

'Of course, you could do that,' I spoke directly to Debbie, determined not to exclude her from the conversation. 'But you'd have to pay for it.'

'No, it's not what—'

'Comes down to money, dunnit?' he demanded.

'Yes,' I agreed.

94

'And she gets you, cut-price, part-time,' he sneered. He craved a reaction but he didn't get one.

I spoke to Debbie again. 'The firm are employing me and you know what I'm paid to do. You've got a right to do anything else you want on top of that. If you do decide to hire security, there are several reputable firms I can put you in touch with. I'm sorry we've not been able to identify him yet, but I'm confident that the next time he's here I'll be able to trace him.'

Ricky snorted.

'I'd better go now,' I said pleasantly. 'Goodbye.'

Debbie got up to see me out, avoiding my eyes and mumbling goodbye. Ricky remained in Action Man pose, stony-faced.

Christ, I thought as I climbed into the car. If Debbie had to put up with his hectoring on top of being stalked, no wonder she was on tablets. Big brother, big help. I shuddered. And in his blustering attempts to protect her he was undermining any chance she had to hold onto her self-esteem.

CHAPTER FOURTEEN

The nursery where Emma Clegg worked was housed in a conversion of one of the grand Victorian villas in Whalley Range. When it was first built, the area was an upmarket suburb for the merchants of Manchester – those doing well in the cotton trade and associated industries. It boasted spacious family housing, tree-lined streets and a grand park nearby.

Nowadays many of the villas are crumbling though the trees are still thriving. I could see the poverty of the area reflected in the dismal row of shops I passed; half of them were boarded up, littered with posters and daubed with graffiti, the others were shabby with neglect, roofs pitted with holes, paint peeling. There was a young prostitute on the corner where I turned; she looked bored and ill tempered.

Emma was waiting for me at the door. We walked along to the park and found a bench with enough wood left on it to support us. There were squirrels and magpies busy chasing each other in the trees, and across the field a group of boys on mountain bikes swooped and wove around each other. The day was turning cooler but it hadn't started to rain. They'd just mown the grass and the smell was intoxicating.

Emma was convinced that Luke Wallace had been wrongly accused. It was refreshing to talk to someone who was keen to help defend him. Nobody had bothered to interview her. Understandable, as she had left the club early on the night of the murder and had no close connection with any of the parties involved.

'They were such good mates, I couldn't believe it when I heard.'

'You can't think of any reason why Luke might attack Ahktar?'

'He wouldn't,' she insisted. 'They never fell out. They were cool. Never a bad word between them. I mean, there's some people always taking the hump or losing their rag, like Zeb, say, foul temper. There's times I had to pull him away from fights.' She shook her head at the memory. 'But Luke and Ahktar, they were as soft as sh—' She blushed. I grinned to reassure her.

She opened her Tupperware lunchbox. Inside were two crisp-breads, a tiny pot of cottage cheese, a spoon and an apple. She took out the cottage cheese and, spooning it onto the crispbread, took a bite. 'You seen Luke?'

'Yes, I went to Golborne.'

'Is he all right?'

'Not really,' I admitted, 'it's not easy for him.'

She nodded, took another bite. I was starving. Should I leave my lunch till later – show solidarity with her diet? Sod it. I unwrapped my sandwich. Was it my fault half the population counted calories?

'Ahktar was stabbed,' I said through my first mouthful, 'but Luke never carried a knife.'

'That's right. And they check for people carrying on the door, run the wand over you.'

'So it would be hard to get in with a knife but not impossible?' I took a second huge bite.

'Nah. I've seen people in there with all sorts. There's ways, I suppose, and say if you know the bouncers they're not going to give you any grief.'

'You said Zeb sometimes got into fights. Would you say he was violent, then?'

She grimaced. 'Short fuse, really, dead moody.'

I recalled his barely suppressed rage.

She glanced at me, frowned. 'He never carried a knife. No,' she shook her head several times, 'it wasn't him. He has his faults, plenty of them, but not that, he'd not do that. He might thump someone but he'd never use anything like a weapon.'

But if he was infuriated and a knife was at hand? Losing his temper, losing control. At that moment was it any different from thumping someone?

'Besides,' she added, 'Ahktar was his cousin and there was no bad feeling between them.'

'OK. Have you any idea who it might have been?'

'I wish I had. It doesn't make sense. Ahktar, he wasn't the sort to get into trouble.' She finished her crispbreads and cheese and took out the apple. 'Someone said there were witnesses, though, someone who saw what happened?'

I nodded. 'Mr and Mrs Siddiq.'

'Siddiq – Rashid Siddiq?' Her eyes widened. She held the apple in mid-air.

'You know him?'

'Yeah, he works for Jay, with Zeb and that.'

My stomach tightened as she talked, alert to the implications of what she was saying. Zeb Khan did know Rashid Siddiq. 'At the Cash and Carry?'

'They've a few places – a warehouse up Cheetham Hill, and they had a shop in the underground market as well. Expect it's shut now.'

'With the bomb,' I bit off another chunk of sandwich, rescued some of the tomato as it slithered out of the side.

'What was he doing at Nirvana?' Emma wondered. 'Shouldn't have thought it was his scene.'

'Too old?'

She blew out, raised her eyebrows. 'Never seen him there before. Not the dancing type.'

And his wife had been very defensive about their

decision to go there that night. 'You didn't see him New Year's Eve?'

'No.'

There was a burst of laughter and jeering from across the park as one of the boys fell and slithered along the ground, his bike on top of him.

'What does Rashid Siddiq do for Jay?'

'Dunno. Bit of a hard man, I reckon, security and that, sort out trouble. He used to come and pick Zeb up now and then. Gave me the creeps.'

I waited for her to elaborate.

'He never had much to say for himself and if you tried small talk he'd just ignore you. Dead rude.'

'Did he know Ahktar?'

She thought about it. 'I expect they'd have bumped into each other at the shop or the warehouse. I know Ahktar went up there now and again. I suppose they'd know each other by sight, but not well, like.'

Not at all, according to the Siddiqs.

'And what does Zeb do at work?'

'As little as possible,' she laughed. 'He and Jay hate each other's guts. Zeb reckons Jay got all the breaks, big brother and that, gets his own business going but Zeb never gets a share in it. He's just an employee, thinks he should be a partner.'

'So Jay's in charge, and Zeb works for him?'

'Yeah, and if it hadn't been for the family, Jay would have slung Zeb out years ago. He's well pissed off with him.'

'Because he doesn't work hard?'

'And he's unreliable and he throws it all away. All the money he makes goes on blackjack or on . . .' She hesitated.

'Cocaine? I know he uses it quite heavily.' Something occurred to me. 'Is he dealing as well?'

'I never asked. He never said.' The way she chose to phrase it made it clear she was ninety-nine per cent certain he was.

'Does Jay know?'

She didn't speak. When I looked at her there was a guarded look in her eyes which had not been there before.

'It might be irrelevant,' I said. 'All of this might be, or it might fit in with something else that helps get Luke off.'

She started as there was a sudden crash of branches and a shriek from the magpie in the trees.

'If anyone knew that I'd told you . . .' she explained with reluctance.

'The only way that could ever happen is if it becomes a vital part of the evidence in Luke's defence. Then you'd be called as a defence witness and you'd have full protection. I'm not interested in drugs, or busting people, that's not why I'm here. It's my job to find out anything I can that casts doubt on Luke murdering Ahktar.'

'What's the connection?' she asked.

'There may not be one, like I said. It could all be irrelevant to the defence but I'd still like to know.'

'Just in case,' she said wryly.

'Yes.'

She sighed. Turned the apple in her hand. 'I couldn't swear to it, I kept well out of it, but you hear things. Jay's business, import/export – well . . . it isn't all clothes and the Cash and Carry stuff. Now and then there'd be a lot of people coming and going, phone calls, stuff Zeb didn't want to talk about. Sometimes he and Rashid would be away a day or two over at Hull or Holyhead or Southampton – where the ports are.' She stopped. 'That's all.'

'Jay was bringing stuff in?'

She bit into the apple. Nodded.

'Was Ahktar involved in any of this?'

'No way,' she said emphatically. 'I know they were cousins but they were really different. Jay and Zeb, I reckon they are mixed up in all sorts. Ahktar – he was studying for his exams, he wasn't interested in any of that.'

I finished the rest of my sandwich while I absorbed what Emma had told me.

'That night, at Nirvana, was Jay there?'

'No. He never goes to places like that. Especially not anywhere Zeb might be. Zeb owed him money, he owed everyone money but Jay wanted paying. Zeb was in a foul mood; he thought he'd have to sell the flat.'

I asked Emma to go over the events of that night as she remembered them. She and Zeb had arrived early at the club, just after half past eight. Zeb sought out Ahktar and gave him the jacket he'd ordered.

'It was only three months late,' she laughed, 'but Ahktar was made up, dancing round in it. Luke's trying to get them side by side, Zeb and Ahktar, like a fashion show. Zeb is in one of his stupid moods so he goes off to the bar. Ahktar was dancing and twirling, he looked great.' Her face fell. Without asking I knew she was thinking about how that evening had ended, with Ahktar's new jacket drenched in his blood.

She told me how she had danced for a while, with Zeb glowering from the sidelines. Joey D had come along and they'd bought some Es off him.

'Got better for a while,' she said, 'then Zeb goes and blows it, asks me for a loan – can he nip to the hole-in-the-wall with my card. I couldn't believe it! I'd paid for my ticket already and now he wanted to borrow off me. You know what I earn? Four-fifty an hour; four-fifty an hour and he's tapping off me. Wanting money. More money. I'd had enough. I'd loaned him before, I'm not tight, but I never saw it again. Oh, he'd take me out to dinner or buy me some flowers and call it quits. I was trying to save for a holiday, for a place of my own, and he was like a drain. I told him to stuff it and I went home. Happy New Year, eh?'

'And after that?'

'Well, he didn't come crawling after me begging

101

forgiveness. Not a word. And I haven't seen him or any of that lot since.'

Emma had left about ten thirty that night. She said she would have gone to Ahktar's funeral but it specified family only. She asked me if I thought Luke would like a visit from her. I assured her he would. Anything that made him feel he was believed and that he was not entirely alone would help his morale.

Before leaving I asked Emma about Joey D. Did she know he'd run away from home?

'No. You don't think he did it, do you?'

'He did have a knife,' I pointed out.

'Yeah, he was like a big kid with it. But Joey,' she shook her head in disbelief, 'oh, he could be a pain but he was that sweet tempered. Either that or thick skinned. I felt sorry for him really.'

'Why?'

I drank my pineapple juice.

'He was like a limpet, clinging on, wanting to get in with everyone but he was just a big kid. He'd always get stuff for us. Couple of times we went to his place – you seen it?' She widened her eyes. 'Mansion. We had parties there. I reckon people took advantage of him, used him. He wanted friends but no one was interested. He only ever got invited anywhere if someone wanted him to bring some drugs.'

'Did he get stuff from Zeb?'

'I don't know.' She frowned. 'He came round the flat a couple of times. I made myself scarce. But he must have had other people for his regular stuff. Joey could get you anything, small-scale, like, but he wasn't in it for the money. It wasn't a business for him, he just liked being able to help people out, I reckon.'

'But with the brothers, Zeb and Jay, that was more serious? They were importing it, after all. Jay was probably setting it up, providing the finance, and sending Zeb along with Rashid Siddiq to collect it.'

'I think.' She stressed the word.

'It was a business to them, they were in it to make a lot of money.'

'Yeah. Least, Jay was. All Zeb ever made was a mess of things.' I drained my drink. Wondered whether any of this talk of drug smuggling had a bearing on the murder.

'Joey D,' I thought aloud. 'His grandmother said he was very frightened, just after the stabbing. That's when he ran away.'

She shrugged. 'Maybe he knows something. Look, if Joey had done it he'd be the sort to give himself up. He'd like all the attention, he'd go for that, picture all over the papers, telly. I can't see it.'

I sighed. Neither could I. I couldn't see anything clearly yet. But there were clues there in what Emma had told me. Threads to pick at and knots to untie in the finicky process of unfolding the truth.

CHAPTER FIFTEEN

I couldn't fathom out why Sonia Siddiq had claimed that Ahktar Khan was a stranger to her and her husband. Surely the witness testimony would be just as valid if Siddiq knew the victim. I tried to find a reason for the denial. Why did it matter? What changed if Rashid Siddiq had known Ahktar Khan? I turned it over and over in my mind but came up blank. Apart from the startlingly obvious conclusion that Rashid Siddiq had wished to obscure the relationship because if it was known about, it could lead to awkward questions.

'OK,' I muttered aloud as I paced my office, 'if Rashid Siddiq has something to hide, then why come forward in the first place?' He could have just left it. Nobody knew that the Siddiqs had seen Ahktar being killed, so why speak out? Conscience? From someone Emma had described as a heavy with involvement in drug smuggling? It didn't add up. My investigation was revealing new facts and the picture was shifting, but it was still jumbled; nothing was in focus, no clear relationship between the different elements.

I was even more bemused by Zeb Khan's clumsy lie, his denial of any contact with Rashid Siddiq. The two men worked together. Whatever was going on, I was sure the fabrication would be well worth exploring in court.

I sat down and wrote a brief report for Mr Wallace outlining who I had spoken to, what points might prove useful for Luke's defence, and what I thought was worth further scrutiny. I also totted up my time and expenses and prepared an invoice.

Hoping he'd be keen to retain me, I listed what further action I'd take: corroborate that Rashid and Ahktar were known to each other and that Rashid and Zeb were colleagues; continue to examine the Siddiqs with the hope of discrediting their reliability; attempt to meet with Joey D; discuss hypnosis with Luke and arrange for it if he agreed; and meet with Dermott Pitt, Luke's lawyer, to tell him what I'd uncovered.

I rang Mr Wallace to arrange a time to meet and he was eager to see me as soon as possible. We fixed on first thing the following morning. I also rang Golborne and booked to see Luke on Monday morning.

Then I went to pick the kids up.

Friday morning and the journey through town was just as laborious as before. Little looked to have changed in the bombed area and we were still diverted, following buses and coaches along small side streets. I saw a poster on a hoarding: *They went for the heart of Manchester but missed the soul. Together we can rebuild our city.* My eyes teared up. I sniffed hard and waited for the queue to move.

Victor Wallace answered the door himself this time. It was a dull damp day so there was no sitting in the garden. No coffee either, as if all he could concentrate on was the case. As soon as we were settled in the study he began to quiz me. 'You said there was new information. Does it exonerate Luke? What does Pitt say?' In his eagerness he was almost hectoring me, his shiny face alert, eyes bright with hope.

'I've brought this,' I handed him my report, 'it summarizes the main points and where I'd like to go next.'

He scanned it, nodding, looking up at me and then back at the paper, his head bobbing to the rhythm of the sentences as though he would memorize them.

'Good, good,' he muttered, then directly at me: 'Good. This is what we need and more of it. Start with Pitt. I'm seeing Luke later today, I'll fill him in but I think you should see him yourself.'

I smiled. 'I took the precaution of booking a visit for Monday. He's agreed to hypnosis too, and I've arranged for someone I know to see him on the Tuesday.'

He frowned momentarily. 'Do you think he'll remember something?'

'Maybe. It can't do any harm, anyway.' Unless Luke did it and he remembers the unthinkable. I kept that possibility to myself.

'Could it stir up . . . he's not very bright at the moment.'

'No. It's a form of relaxation; it should help. She's very good, the woman I know. I trust her. She said you can't make someone say or do anything they don't want to; the patient's got to feel safe and comfortable.'

'And he's agreed to it, you say?'

I nodded. 'He rang last night.'

'OK.' He turned back to the papers. 'I'm not clear exactly on this stuff about the eye-witnesses. They said they didn't know Ahktar but you think they did?'

'Well, Rashid did, certainly. I don't know about Mrs Siddiq.'

'Is it important?'

'Only because it's a discrepancy. It might help discredit them. If they've lied about that, what else might they have lied about? It shows they are less than honest.'

'Why would they do that?'

I shrugged. 'I'm still trying to figure it out. It could be a red herring.'

'But this business with the Deason boy should set some alarm bells ringing?'

'I'd have thought so. Although at the time the police were happy to leave it, once his grandmother showed them his knife and they knew it wasn't the murder weapon. Now he's been away so long, maybe we can interest them in why he ran and what scared him so much he's not come back.'

He grunted assent, still referring to my notes.

'I'm interested in Zeb Khan too,' I said. 'He claims to have seen the lads quarrelling that night. It gives the prosecution some motive, but he was the only one to see it. Plus he lied outright when I asked if he knew Rashid Siddiq. They work together, according to Emma, Zeb's ex-girlfriend. Zeb owed money, quite a lot apparently. Emma said he was thinking of selling his flat, he was a regular drug-user and may even have been involved in supplying drugs. We know he was on drugs that night.'

'They all were, weren't they,' he said bitterly.

'But there should be plenty of scope to undermine his testimony,' I persisted. 'I don't think there was any argument; I think he made it up afterwards to fit the facts. Nobody else could believe it. He believes Luke killed his cousin, and he wants justice.'

'It's not justice if it's the wrong person,' Mr Wallace burst out.

'You don't need to convince me.'

'God, I'm sorry. But there is some hope. I was afraid,' he took a deep breath and sighed, 'I was afraid you'd come back and tell me there was nothing you could do.'

'There are chinks. No more than that yet, but it's a start, something to work away at.'

He paid my invoice and I promised to let him know if anything significant cropped up. Before leaving I asked him for a photo of Luke.

'There's this one, it's the most recent.' It was the band, the photo that had been in the newspaper. Luke and Ahktar were in the middle, by the drums, the other boys Josh and Simon to right and left. They weren't smiling, but I suppose they were aiming for one of those moody boy-band poses.

'They had loads of those made up like postcards with some stuff on the back so people could ring up and book them. They'd played a couple of times at school.'

'Were they any good?'

He shrugged, smiled ruefully. 'They thought so, and their friends liked it. I used to play, when I was Luke's age – guitar.' He cleared his throat. I thought he was embarrassed that he'd told me but then he carried on: 'I can't bear it, you know, him in there, all this. It's tearing me apart. I feel so . . . so damn useless.' His voice rose with frustration. 'I can't do anything for him. I can't look after him. I'm his father and yet I can't stop it happening. What it's doing to him, watching him change . . . Christ, how can I ever make it better?'

His eyes glittered as he held my look. I recalled the moment when Dr Khan had told me about identifying Ahktar's body. The grief stretching his eyes wide.

There was no answer.

There was something else I wanted to work away at or someone. Mrs Deason's face changed from polite enquiry to dismay when she saw me on the doorstep. Her shoulders stiffened and for a second I thought she was going to close the door in my face. She didn't; however, nor did she invite me in. I don't know whether it was the rain or the worry, but she looked careworn and the brisk energy I'd enjoyed on our first meeting had drained away.

'Have you asked Joey if he'll talk to me?'

'He's frightened.'

Of what? 'He can't hide for ever. Does he know about Luke, about the trial?'

She nodded, her eyes failing to meet mine, wanting to be anywhere but here.

'Has he told you what he's frightened of, who he's frightened of?'

She shook her head, swallowed.

I took the photo from my pocket. 'This is Ahktar and this is Luke. Did you ever meet them? I know Joey brought friends home sometimes; they had parties here, I believe. Luke's finding it very hard, being locked up. He's depressed. His father's worried sick. Imagine the shock; your best mate is dead and you're awaiting trial for murder. Can't even go to his funeral. He's a nice boy, Luke. He's had a lot to cope with already, you know. His Mum died when he was twelve, now this.'

She turned her head away, compressed her lips.

'Please, Mrs Deason, ask Joey again. Remember, I'm not working for the authorities. I can meet him wherever he wants, hear what he has to say. I still won't know where he is hiding, but I may be able to help Luke.'

No response.

I put the photo away. 'It won't be all that long,' I said, ''till I have to report my findings to the defence lawyers. They may want to follow things up. It could soon move out of my hands. It might be easier for Joey to see me now than have the police looking for him.'

Her face became cold and blank at the threat.

'You've got my number,' I said. 'You can ring any time.'

Some things just fall into place. It doesn't happen often and there's nothing quite like it – it makes my blood sing. I don't know whether it's luck or destiny, or whether it's down to me. But it makes up for all the dead ends and the diversions, all the cold leads and the false starts.

On that Friday morning I took a wrong turning as I drove away from Mrs Deason's house, and instead of heading back towards Manchester I found I was going the other way, bound for Bury.

I wrestled with the glove compartment to find my A–Z and pulled into the roadside so I could plot a route back. I was only five minutes from the well-appointed Deason home but already the territory had changed. This was a much poorer area; the terraces along the road had doors opening straight onto the pavement. The place looked tired and drab and hard up. Few of the occupants had bothered to clean their windows or wash their nets, though here and there one stood out smart with new paint, glowing white curtains, silk flowers or doll in full Flamenco gear on the windowsill, highlighting the shabbiness of the neighbouring houses.

I took the next side street, intending to go round the block and back to the main road. Some of the houses had been converted into shops. A grocer's and off-licence on one corner, Betty's Hair Salon on another. I passed a small row of shops further on – chip shop, bookies, video shop and at the end of the row *A.J. Henson's Knives for Crafts, Sport and Leisure.*

I stopped the car and sat there for a few moments. Let my theory filter down like a marble on some complicated run, clunk, clunk, clunk.

Inside the shop, everything was displayed in shiny lock-up cases or chained up on the wall in amongst hunting memorabilia. Dusty stuffed birds perched on plinths and fish that could have been carved out of wood but were probably pickled in lacquer hung stiff and dull from the ceiling. In pride of place above the counter hung a huge tiger's head, mouth bared, teeth exposed. I felt a wave of nausea for the mentality that continued to display the trophy while the tiger itself faced extinction. I thought of Maddie's awkward questions when we watched wildlife programmes. 'But why do they kill them, Mummy? That's so mean.'

Why? Because some people enjoy hunting down animals, because some people are starving, because . . .

The tiger was incongruous too in this backwater of north Manchester. These beasts had never prowled round Collyhurst or roared from the hills in Heaton Park.

The buzzer that had sounded when I went into the shop

brought a man out from the back. He was small and bespec-
tacled, with black greasy hair and bland, casual clothes.

He smiled. 'Can I help?'

Sometimes it's best to tell the truth. I showed him one
of my cards. 'I'm a private investigator. I'm working on a
case involving people in the area. I'm afraid I can't go into
details, but I'm interested in any records you have of knife
sales over the Christmas and New Year period.'

He pulled a face. 'We don't have any sort of stock breakdown like that.'

I tried another tack.

'Do you remember selling a knife to an elderly woman,
early in the New Year? She was probably well dressed, and
had a Southern accent.'

He pursed his lips, shook his head. My theory teetered
like a tower of blocks. Shit. I turned to go. 'Is there anyone
else works here?'

He drew a breath. He didn't like my persistence but it
was laziness rather than obstruction.

He put his head through the door behind the counter.
'Carla?'

Carla emerged – young, plump, apple-cheeked with a
set of rings and studs in her nostrils. There was a tension
between the two of them which made me slightly embarrassed. Had I interrupted something? It would more than
explain his reluctance to indulge me in my search and pro-
long my stay.

I described Mrs Deason as best I could to Carla. Did she
remember her buying a knife?

'Oh, yeah,' she didn't hesitate. 'she had the name written down and everything. A late Christmas present for her
nephew, she said.'

'You've a good memory,' I complimented her.

'Well,' she demurred, 'she stuck out a bit really. We get
mainly lads in or anglers, you know.'

'How did she pay?'

'Cash, I think.'

'Can you remember when it was?'

'First day back after the holiday. Would have been the second of January.' She glanced at Mr Henson for confirmation.

He nodded. 'I was at the suppliers,' he chipped in. 'Carla was on her own for the morning.'

Mrs Deason had made her purchase just in the nick of time. The police had called on her that very same afternoon, to check on Joey's knife.

'I reckon she was the only person came in,' said Carla. 'That's another reason I remember – it was dead as a graveyard.'

'No one's ever got any money after Christmas,' he observed.

I took down the details of the knife that Mrs Deason had bought and Mr Henson showed me a model. It was bigger than I remembered, with a broad, slightly curved blade and a horn handle.

I felt a little eddy of giddiness as I imagined the damage it could do. Thought of it slicing through Ahktar's jacket. One cut, one move, one moment – that was all it had taken.

CHAPTER SIXTEEN

I contained my sense of excitement until I was back in the car and then I clenched my fists in triumph. 'Yes! Yes! Yes!' Things were finally moving.

I considered all the way home how I would break the news to Mrs Deason. And should I? Was it more or less likely that Joey would agree to see me if I revealed that I knew about the knife? It implicated him full square for Ahktar's murder. I reasoned that if he had done it, then he was on the run and wouldn't agree to meet me whatever I said. I remembered Emma's view, he'd want the publicity, but there were other ways of getting that. He'd run till they trapped him, then enact some final glorious gesture; Bonnie and Clyde, Sid Vicious. Or maybe a guilty conscience would overcome him once the trial got under way, and he'd come riding back and into court with testimony to prevent the wrong man being convicted.

Emma could have got it wrong. The instinct for self preservation's strong, and maybe Joey would just sit it out and watch while Luke Wallace was tried.

Past experience had taught me that once the wheels of the criminal justice system are set in motion, it can be very difficult to call a halt, even with startling new evidence. My information about the knives might not convince people to drop the case against Luke, or go off hunting for Joey D, but I was certain it would prove a strong part of Luke's defence.

And if Joey D was innocent, why was he hiding? I reminded myself that it was not my responsibility to find out who killed Ahktar Khan, but only to find out whether Luke Wallace could be cleared. And things were looking up.

I stopped in Withington on the way to my office and deposited the cheque from Victor Wallace in my account. It was all already spoken for – rent, bills, birthday present for Tom, new trainers for Maddie. My own treat was limited to a modest takeaway lunch from the Health Food shop. Spinach bhaji and chocolate flapjack. 'Go on,' a voice whispered in my head, 'get yourself some perfume. You need some new clothes, too, and a bit of bath essence won't break the bank,' but I resisted. Next pay cheque, I told myself. Maybe then. I resisted all the way back to the car. I'd even got the key in the lock. Then I turned, retraced my steps and splashed out on a pair of earrings, a velvet leopard-print scarf and some vanilla body cream. I grinned all the way to work.

A proper coffee machine would have improved my modest working conditions but I hadn't got there yet; I had to make do with instant coffee instead. Once back in the office I put the kettle on and wolfed down my food.

Did the plants need a drink, too?

I gave the cactus garden on top of the filing cabinet a small amount of water.. I'd tried keeping plants in the office before but even geraniums mutinied and died; just not enough regular loving care. I reckoned cacti were a good bet; after all, it is quite hard to tell when a cactus has perished – a good year or so to realize that they're not growing . . .

The phone rang. 'He's gonna kill me! Help me, I know he is! He's gonna kill me!' She was hysterical.

'Debbie!' I spoke sharply, trying to interrupt her whirl of panic. 'Are you at home?'

114

'Yeah, and he's . . . he's . . .' The note of hysteria began to rise again.

'Where is he?'

'Outside. I can't go out, the kids, I've got to get the kids. I can't go out, he's waiting,' she whimpered.

'Which school?'

'St John's.'

'What road is it on?'

'Chepstow, off Longford Road.'

'Listen, I'll ring them, I'll tell the school that you'll be late. Stay there, wait for me, I'm coming now. Do you understand? I'll make sure they keep the kids at school. They'll be OK. Do you understand?'

'Yes.' She began to cry. I put the phone down.

Oh hell. What about Maddie and Tom? I rang Nana 'Tello, Ray's mother, no reply. None of the Dobsons were in, I nipped upstairs to double-check. I sometimes asked Vicky, the eldest daughter, to babysit.

I locked up and drove round the corner to home. Ran over the road. Denise was in and yes, she could collect Maddie and Tom when she went for her daughter. I thanked her with feeling. I wasn't sure when I'd be back, but Ray would be home by six. No problem. Back home I scribbled a note for Ray explaining what I'd arranged. I found the number for St John's in the phone book and when I got through I told them that Debbie Gosforth had been delayed and would be late picking up Connor, Jason and their sister.

'I'll be collecting her in the car and giving her a lift to school so we shouldn't be all that late.'

I was relieved that the secretary didn't press for more details. I didn't want to reveal that Debbie was being stalked before checking with her.

Ten past three and half of Manchester clambers into cars to go and fetch the children. They were all going from Withington to Chorlton that day. Maybe more than usual

115

in the face of the soft rain that continued to seep endlessly from the bright, blank skies.

I worked hard to relax on the journey over. Being strung out wouldn't get me there any quicker, wouldn't help Debbie.

He was there. I parked right outside her house in Ivy-green Road and looked over at him. He was still, as before, his hands clasped in front of him, eyes fixed on the house. I was tempted to go over and ask him outright what the hell he thought he was doing, but my priority at that moment was to make sure Debbie was safe.

I hammered on the door then called through the letter box. 'Debbie, it's me, Sal. Open the door.'

I couldn't hear anything. 'Debbie, open the door! Debbie!' I bawled. It was impossible to see through the letter box; little brushes lined the opening to keep out dust and draughts and prying eyes. I peered in through the lounge window but the nets obscured any view of the room within. I ran back to the car and used my mobile to ring her number. It rang and rang. No one answered it.

My chest tightened. Where was she? Had she done something stupid? He stood across the road. Watching. I walked along to the next alleyway between the rows of houses and went down it to the rear of her house. The back gate to Debbie's place was ajar; the back door open. I didn't like it, I didn't like it at all.

I hurried inside. No sign in the kitchen.

'Debbie!' I kept calling her name. The lounge was deserted. I didn't want to go upstairs. My throat was dry. I couldn't hear any sounds – no crying, no breathing. Only the chatter of sparrows outside and the ebb and flow of traffic. I climbed the stairs.

The bathroom was empty. Towels folded neatly on the radiator, bath toys held in a bright red net bag slung over the taps. The top was on the toothpaste tube.

There were three other doors. All closed.

'Debbie?' It was almost a whisper. I cleared my throat and spoke up. 'Debbie?' Silence.

I opened the first door. Bunk beds, pink curtains, Spice Girls posters. No Debbie.

The second. Apricot walls, white cover on the bed, built-in wardrobe. Could she be hiding in there? 'Debbie?' I braced myself, slid back the door. Skirts, blouses, suits all neatly hung. Shoes paired. Jumpers folded.

One more door. The boys' room.

I heard knocking, downstairs, the front door. My heart tried to get out. I ran to the window and peered out. He'd moved, was no longer standing sentinel across the street. Shit.

Go and answer it then, you twerp. My thumping heart wouldn't quite knuckle under. I took a couple of deep breaths then walked downstairs quite normally.

'Hello?' I spoke to the door. 'Who is it?' No reply. I turned the Yale but couldn't open it. Of course, she kept it locked.

I heard a sound then – tiny, from the back. Oh God, he was coming in the back! The kitchen door was shut. I couldn't see through it. I didn't want to be trapped upstairs. I moved as quietly as I could into the lounge. Stood right behind the door, pressed against the wall. I heard the squeak of the kitchen door handle, the door being pulled open. There was silence as he listened and I listened, and my knee tremored uncontrollably. He was trying to work out where I was. Did he know that he was stalking the wrong woman? Would I be all right if I showed myself? My mind whipped through the options while the seconds stretched and the silence grew louder:

Wait to be found? Hope he'll give up and go? Jump out wailing like a banshee and hope he'll flee? Yes. I raised my hands ready to shove the door and leap.

Then a child's voice cracked the silence. 'Uncle Ricky, hiya.'

Footsteps, hubbub. Clattering sounds, voices.

I let my hands fall. Stepped from behind the door and out of the lounge to find Ricky and Debbie's daughter in the hall. He looked at me in astonishment. Behind him, in the kitchen, I saw Debbie and the boys, laden with bags and lunchboxes.

I took a couple of paces forward, stared at her.

'Oh, hiya,' she looked pale and shaky but she smiled and laughed nervously.

'Debbie,' I said 'I asked you to wait here. I didn't know where you'd gone.'

Ricky frowned, glanced from me to his sister.

'I got here and the back door was wide open and he was still there across the street.'

Ricky moved towards the front door.

'He's gone now,' I snapped, 'and I didn't get a chance to go after him because you called me and I thought you needed my help, and when I get here it's like the Marie Celeste and you're nowhere to be found.'

'I had to get the children,' she chewed on her chain.

'I rang the school,' I said 'as I promised I would. I asked you to wait, said we'd go together. I didn't know what had happened to you. You left the door wide open, you know, anyone could have walked in.'

'Sorry,' she giggled again breathlessly and smiled at me. But her eyes were bright with fear. 'I'm fine now.'

Much as I admired the reserves of strength she must have summoned to get herself out of the house in that state and collect her kids, I still had one overwhelming impulse towards Debbie Gosforth.

I wanted to slap her face.

I had a look round the nearby streets in case I could see the stalker's car, but had no joy.

Back at Debbie's the children were watching television and Debbie and Ricky were in the kitchen. I sat down and accepted a cup of tea. Then I collected some more details from her.

The phone calls had continued. She was following the phone company's advice; they would monitor the situation, see if he got tired of the lack of reaction. There had been another letter. She handed it to me with trembling fingers. The spiky, black writing added an edge to the venomous sentiments expressed. At times he'd pressed so hard that the paper was torn. G quoted some Biblical passages about harlots and vengeance, and went on to claim that Debbie had betrayed their love and tried to destroy him. *I will get you*, he had written, the words underlined several times for effect. *Slag, whore, sister of Jezebel. I will cut off your breasts, rip out your tongue.*

'Oh God, this is horrible.' I handed the first page to Ricky.

G ended with a plea for reconciliation. *I can forgive you, Debbie, and destiny can find its way and our true love shine. Don't let them poison your mind any more. Don't let them strangle our love. You know in your heart that what you are doing is wrong. Debbie, my love is a flame that will never die. Now that I have found you I will never let you go. WE WILL BE TOGETHER. G*

I sighed and passed Ricky page two.

I had to push and prompt to get Debbie to talk. She had noticed him watching the house as she returned from shopping early that afternoon. He'd approached her. As she got to that part of her story, she began to tremble violently, almost unable to speak. Ricky shifted in his seat, tried to take her hand but her hands flew here and there touching the studs in her ears, grazing the chain, patting her hair.

She laughed incongruously. 'He said he'd been waiting. He—' She stopped abruptly, and her face went blank. 'Are you staying for tea, Ricky?' Her brother was as nonplussed as me. 'I've got lasagne in the freezer.'

'Debbie,' I said gently, 'did he touch you?'

She looked at me crossly. I was an irritation.

'What did he do? I need to write it down, for evidence.'

'I didn't do anything!' she exclaimed.

'I know. You haven't done anything wrong. This man is frightening you, that's why I'm here. What he is doing is wrong. We want to stop him. What did he do?'

Her hands lighted on her hair, her chain again, then she crossed them round her neck. 'He held me.'

'Like, that round your neck?'

'He kissed me.' She began to cry.

'Jesuschrist,' Ricky swore and stood up abruptly.

'I'm sorry,' she wailed.

'Debbie, it's all right. He shouldn't have done that; it's an assault, it's not your fault. Debbie?' She looked up at me. 'Did he do anything else?' She shook her head.

'What he did, that's a criminal offence, he can be charged.'

'Mum.' A child's voice from the lounge.

She stood quickly, wiped her face roughly with her hands, and went through to the lounge.

'Ricky?' He stood with his back to me, arms braced on the edge of the sink looking out to the backyard. 'Your sister needs to see her doctor. She can't take this.'

'Bastard!' He banged his fist on the edge of the sink.

'I know. Look, she shouldn't be on her own. Can you stay with her? Is there anyone else?'

He nodded. 'I'll be here.' He turned to face me. 'If he comes within a mile of this place I'll smash his fucking face in. I'll do for him, I will.'

'I can see how you feel but that's not what Debbie needs at the moment,' I told him. 'She needs to feel safer, calmer. Maybe there's somewhere else she could stay, her and the kids. She needs to get out of here till we've sorted this guy out. She's cracking up.' I emphasized it.

'What d'you expect?' He rounded on me. 'First she's in the bomb, that does her head in, then this pervert.'

'I know,' I retorted, 'but the best you can do is to just get her some help. Take her to a doctor, get her out of here.

120

Don't keep ranting on about the stalker and what you'll do to him. Concentrate on her. Ring me when you've sorted something out.'

He glared at me for a moment then nodded. 'What about . . . ?'

He jerked his head towards the front of the house.

'If there's any sign, ring me. I'm going to brief the neighbours, ask them to look out too.'

'If you'd followed him today . . .' he began sulkily.

'I couldn't. I had Debbie in hysterics on the phone and when I found that door open I didn't know what to expect, what she might have done to herself.'

He looked at me. The prospect of suicide appalled him. 'Nah.' He shook his head then laughed dismissively. 'Nah, Debbie would never do anything like that.'

'Maybe not, but she's ill. She's cracking up, Ricky.'

Debbie came in then. I told her I'd be asking the neighbours to look out for the stalker and let me know when he returned. I said that Ricky had promised to stay with her for the time being. I left it up to him to discuss moving out for a while. Then I asked her where her tablets were.

She looked confused, went out and returned with a bottle. I read the label. 'Have you had any today?'

She appeared to think about it then her face became dreamy and vague. I checked the date and counted out the tablets. By my reckoning, she'd missed three doses.

'Take one now,' I suggested, 'it'll make you feel better.' She complied.

'I'm fine,' she said, her smile trembling. 'Just fine.' Then her hands began to dance again.

CHAPTER SEVENTEEN

'Mrs Deason? Sal Kilkenny here.' An intake of breath. 'I haven't had a chance—' she began querulously.

'There's something you should know. Something you should tell Joey. I've found out about the knife – the new knife.'

'I don't know what on earth you mean,' she said. Automatic reflex. It sounded hollow. She knew it; I knew it.

'When Joey came home from the club that night, he didn't have his knife with him. It had been used to kill Ahktar Khan.'

'No!'

'Joey ran away. You knew about the knife. You replaced it, you wanted to protect him. They remember you at Henson's, the knife shop.'

There was silence on the other end of the phone.

'I need to see Joey,' I said.

'He didn't do it,' her words were choked.

'I need to talk to Joey. Soon. Once the lawyers hear about this they'll likely call the police back in, and it'll be out of my hands. This is a murder enquiry, Mrs Deason, and you deliberately misled the police about the murder weapon. I don't know whether Joey is up to his neck in it, or an innocent bystander, but he won't be able to hide for much longer. Ask him whether he'd rather talk to me first or wait for the police to come.' I waited in case she wanted to say anything. There was nothing. I put the phone down.

I tried Victor Wallace but he'd left the answerphone on. He was visiting Luke that afternoon; maybe still on his way back. I left a message for him to call me when he had a moment.

Finally I rang Mr Pitt's office. His secretary said he had left for the weekend and would be tied up in court till the middle of the next week. I explained that I had some significant new information regarding the Luke Wallace case. I could meet him at the courts if that would make things any easier. She promised to pass the message on as soon as possible.

I suppose in the scale of things it didn't make a great deal of difference to Dermott Pitt whether he acted on the new information immediately and tried to get the CPS to drop the case, or whether he waited until it came to court when he could demolish the prosecution case, get Luke released and win plaudits into the bargain. In fact, the latter course would probably enhance his reputation and advance his career more.

But it made a massive difference to Luke. The more weeks and months he spent incarcerated at Golborne, the more damage would be done. He was already losing his sense of worth, his sense of purpose, becoming depressed and withdrawn. The consequences could affect him for years to come. He could kiss his youth goodbye. I determined that I would get to see Dermott Pitt early in the week. If necessary I'd hover around the courts. Create enough of a nuisance value and he'd listen to me just to get shut of me.

Friday night, kids asleep, I was wrapping up a pass-the-parcel game, inserting super bouncing balls, dinosaurs that could squirt water, tattoos and face-paints between the layers of paper. Ray was labelling party bags with the guest list and getting muddled as to which bags had got which novelties in. Digger had been banished to the kitchen after showing too much interest in the sweets.

123

'I just hope it's dry,' I said, 'if we can keep them in the garden it'll be ten times easier.'

Ray grunted.

The phone rang. It was Victor Wallace. He was over the moon when I told him about the replacement knife. He demanded I see Pitt right away, asked if I'd told the police yet, was all for calling the press in. I tried to calm him down a bit. I didn't want either police or press at this stage. I was still hoping that I could see Joey D and find out what had actually gone on that night. And it would be wise to see the lawyer with the fresh evidence before doing anything else, as he would be more of an expert in how to use it. I got Victor's agreement on this and accepted his effusive thanks, hoping that they weren't misplaced.

Tom is usually a very equable child with an adventurous spirit. Unlike Maddie he enjoys new situations and challenges, while she hangs back convinced that 'there be monsters' in any fresh environment. But the strains of his fifth birthday party pushed him to the limit.

He held it together for the first highly exciting half hour while he ripped open carefully wrapped presents and tore open cards with signatures laboriously scrawled by his little friends. He coped fairly well with the ensuing games of Pin the Tail on the Dinosaur and Hunt the Treasure in the garden, even though two of his bigger pals knocked him down in their determination to find more sweets than anyone else.

However, anyone who knew him could see signs of mounting tension in his clenched fists and increasingly glazed eyes as he lurched around during Musical Bumps. And when Daniel Metcalfe began to tease Tom over the birthday tea with a typically cruel playground chant: Tom Costello is a smello, and Maddie, o traitorous one, hooted with laughter, then Tom really lost it. He knocked over

Daniel's Cola, yelled at everyone to go home now, dissolved into tears and ran off to his room.

Intense negotiations finally resulted in his return after he'd been promised that he could work the music for Pass the Parcel. The admiration that greeted Sheila's Tyrannosaurus cake helped as well.

'I'm shagged.' Ray staggered into the kitchen having parcelled off the last small guest with a party bag. 'How many more years of this do we have to go through?'

'Five or six,' muttered Sheila with feeling born from experience. 'It gets worse – seven and eight are the pits.' She scraped jelly into the bin. 'Once they hit ten it's a few friends to the pictures or ice-skating.'

'No more party bags,' I said, 'it was a nightmare finding things that were cheap enough and wouldn't break before they got them home.'

'In my day,' Sheila said, 'it was a piece of cake and a balloon. And only one of you got a prize in Pass the Parcel. None of this prize in every layer and stop the music to make sure everyone gets one,' she laughed. 'Awful really, all the bitter disappointment when you didn't win.'

After snacking on cheese and pineapple kebabs, veggie sausages on sticks and jelly, I didn't feel hungry enough to cook a big meal and neither did the others. It was dry and warm even if it was overcast, so we decided to have a picnic in the garden. Sheila had some hummus and cheese, I made a salad, Ray boiled some eggs and heated up some pitta bread, I opened a bottle of chilled white wine.

Maddie and Tom were busy playing with his new acquisitions and ate on the hoof.

It was rare to share a meal with Sheila, who as our lodger led a fairly independent life. She was in her first year of a geology degree and enjoying it immensely. Term was practically over and she was planning a summer travelling round – a mixture of study and socializing.

'I'll start up in Scotland, at Dominic's,' she referred to

her younger son. 'He's kept his flat on and St Andrews will be a great base for touring. I'll do a few of the cities then head off to the highlands.'

I groaned with envy, 'I need a holiday.'

'Thought you were going camping,' said Ray.

'Maddie, get off that trellis.' I waited till she obeyed me. 'Yes, I need to sort something out, borrow a tent, see if Bev and Harry can lend me theirs.'

My old friends and their three boys lived a couple of miles away in Levenshulme. We'd all squashed into that tent on shared holidays when Maddie and Sam and David had been tiny.

'It's mine!' Tom's shriek rent the air. He clung to his new scooter, Maddie stood astride it.

'You've got to share, Tom.' Maddie cast a guilty glance our way.

'C'mon, Maddie, it's his birthday present. Get your own bike out.'

'I hate my bike, it's horrible.' She let go of the scooter which fell, but not on Tom, and wandered off to sit on the swing at the other end of the garden. Tom lifted his scooter up and stood uncertain what to do with it now he'd won sole possession. He could not yet scoot. Once he judged Maddie far enough away to pose no immediate threat, he ran to join her.

The phone broke into the conversation. I looked at Ray. 'It won't be for me,' he insisted.

'Hello?'

'I want Sal Kilkenny.'

'Speaking.'

'That boy that was killed, Ahktar Khan, you've been asking questions about it.' A woman's voice, my age or younger.

'That's right.'

'Well, that witness, Sonia Siddiq, she wasn't there. She's lying – she never saw anything, she can't have done.'

126

Mancunian accent but with a tinge to the words that made me think she was Asian.

'Who is this?' I asked. No reply. 'How do you know she wasn't there? Do you know where Mrs Siddiq was, that night?'

'She wasn't at the club. She's been told to say it – it's not right, she's lying.' The phone went dead.

I sat down trying to digest what I'd just heard. It made sense. It made so much sense when I thought of Mrs Siddiq's attitude, the questions that had troubled her, the delay in coming forward. What about him, though? The caller had only talked about Sonia. Emma had been astonished that Rashid had been at Nirvana. Had he? Had either of them?

But an anonymous phone call – untraceable, impossible to corroborate. A mixed blessing. Progress though. *She's lying*.

Outside it had started to spot with rain. The picnic was over.

CHAPTER EIGHTEEN

On the way to see Luke at the remand centre I played with scenarios in my head. The club, kids tripping, happy. Joey, running round with a little something for everyone, knife tucked away. Ahktar and Luke partying, Zeb irritable and pressed for cash, Emma storming off. Rashid Siddiq, on his own? Out of place, looking like some of the hired help?

Joey stabbing Ahktar, a bad trip, seeing monsters instead of his friend. Luke holding Ahktar, too drugged to cope, to stay awake. Ecstasy wires you up, lets you dance all night, but they'd taken all sorts, hadn't they? Maybe the drugs had been bad, cut with something nasty? Or a dodgy combination powerful enough to make someone psychotic for a while?

I wiped the image clean and started again. Suppose the lads had argued, what then? Joey, eager to help, slipping Luke the knife. 'Here Luke, you show him this, soon shut him up.' Luke, out of it, takes the handle, stumbles. Surprise as Ahktar pitches forward, blood spilling. It wasn't meant to be this way. Joey watching, clocking it, running. Rashid Siddiq walks on by.

With a chill in my guts I realized that there really was no guarantee that Joey's account would exonerate Luke. Joey might not even know what had happened – only that his knife had gone and a young man lay dead. But it must be more than that, surely, to send him so far for so long?

We met in the same grim cubicle as before. Luke looked pinched and pale; he'd lost weight and the nervousness I'd noticed had given way to a dull apathy. He seemed to be half-asleep. I told him about Mrs Deason buying a new knife from Henson's. He frowned in concentration. 'You think Joey did it?'

'I think his knife was used. That's the only reason she'd go out and buy a new one, and it partly accounts for him doing a runner. Though I think there's more to it than that.'

He blinked a couple of times and shook his head. I wondered whether he was getting some sort of sedative, he seemed so dull.

'We don't have to convict anyone else,' I said. 'We just need to make the charge against you look doubtful. I've seen Emma, she wanted to know how you were.' He looked mildly surprised at that. 'She's convinced you're innocent. She split up with Zeb that night, hasn't seen anyone since, but she had some interesting things to tell me. Your dad probably mentioned it. Emma said Rashid Siddiq worked with Zeb and would have known Ahktar, by sight if nothing else. So the Siddiqs have been lying about whether they knew Ahktar, and Zeb Khan has been lying as well, claiming he didn't know Siddiq. For some reason he wants to make a secret of it. Emma also told me that the brothers are involved in drugs, importing stuff. Zeb and Rashid Siddiq collect the stuff and distribute it. You're not surprised?'

'Ahktar said something once, how they were getting into deep water. He knew it was happening but he never had anything to do with it. They were family, so I suppose he heard stuff but he kept his distance. Zeb is a jerk anyway.'

'Emma says he owed Jay money.'

'He owed everyone money,' Luke said, 'but what's all this got to do with me and what happened to Ahktar?'

If only I knew. 'There's something else which makes

129

me more sure that there is a connection,' I went on. 'I got a phone call on Saturday, an anonymous one. The caller said that Mrs Siddiq had not been at Nirvana that night, that her statement was all lies. That someone had told her what to say.'

Luke looked at me, struggling to work out what I meant.

'I've no proof,' I said, 'but it fits with what I've heard so far. When I saw her she got very defensive about the details of that evening – innocent stuff about where they'd sat and who they'd seen. If she's perjured herself, it's good news for you as their testimony is the biggest part of the case against you. There's no motive, after all.'

'What about him?'

'If all I've heard is true, Rashid Siddiq is a very nasty piece of work. He's employed as a minder, security man, whatever, by Jay and every so often he's involved in drug smuggling. According to Emma, he drives down to Southampton or up to Hull or over to Holyhead with Zeb and they collect a little something for Jay. Now, this hard man sees a crime committed. He does nothing at the time but late the next day he's at the police station offering himself up as a witness. To me, that's a bit peculiar. Most people in his position wouldn't go anywhere near the police. They don't want to be known to the police.'

'Maybe he's an informer,' he said.

'It's possible.' I thought about it, 'OK, suppose he is informing on the drug stuff. They'll be after the big players, won't they – the suppliers overseas as well as Jay. if they're using Siddiq, they're not going to want him attracting attention by getting involved as a model citizen in a murder trial. That would only make Jay suspicious, wouldn't it? Because it comes back to it being out of character.'

Luke rubbed his hands over his head, tired of all the supposition. 'It's all "if this" and "maybe that" and "what if" – and yet I'm still fucking here.' His voice rose in

130

desperation. 'Can't you just get me out of here? Can't you just . . .' He covered his face with his hands.

I waited a moment. This place was crushing him: the harsh regime, the pervading culture of hard men and bad boys, the smell, the ceaseless noise, the constant bullying.

'I'm sorry. I realize how hard this must be, being in here. We are making progress,' I said gently. 'I'm going to see Pitt. Think about it: so far we've found new evidence about the murder weapon – Joey D's knife killed Ahktar, the witnesses are lying about knowing him, and one if not both of them is lying about the whole thing. I'm sure Pitt can use this, Luke.'

He didn't respond.

'I'm pushing very hard to see Joey. His grandmother is in touch with him. He knows something, that's why he's hiding. I've given them an ultimatum: me now or the police will be after him. And you're seeing Eleanor tomorrow for the hypnosis.'

'Yeah,' he said gruffly. He looked up at me then, dry-eyed, vulnerable. 'What do you think happened?'

I took a breath, sat up in my seat. It could be dangerous to speculate as he wanted me to, raise false hopes or paint an untrue version of events, but he needed something to hold on to. 'I don't think you killed Ahktar; I don't believe you even argued with him. I think someone else killed him, with Joey's knife. I don't know why Zeb would lie about you two arguing, or why Mrs Siddiq would pretend she was there if she wasn't, or why Rashid Siddiq wanted to stand up and be counted, but I don't think you did it.'

'And the hypnosis. What if it comes out that I did do it? What if it was me?' He shivered.

'Luke, you don't have to go ahead with it, if it's too much, if the time's not right.'

'No, I will. If I can just remember . . . It's the not remembering. You start to think – well, maybe I did do it. I could've done anything.'

'Yes. The hypnosis – she won't get you to remember anything that you don't want to.'

He looked puzzled.

'She said it's got to be relaxed and comfortable – she'll take it gently. I think you'll be fine, but if you start blocking things out or get upset, Eleanor will stop. She's not going to take you any further than you want to go. And you can change your mind; now, in the morning, whenever. OK?'

I let the guard know we had finished and waited while Luke was escorted away. The guard returned for me and took me through to the main entrance.

Outside it was a warm summer's day. There was a border of shrubs around the car park, purple hebe full of pointed flowers and a mock orange blossom shedding white petals with a sweet, tangy scent. There was a carton of juice in the car. I wound the window down so I could smell the air and watch the bees busy combing the hebe while I had my drink.

I watched the bees but I saw Luke lying in his cell waiting for the morning, wondering if the hypnosis would prove his innocence or seal his guilt. And there was a question still to be answered that floored me every time it came to me; if Luke had done it, what on earth was I going to do?

CHAPTER NINETEEN

I pulled into a petrol station on the drive back and rang Dermott Pitt. When I had finally bought a mobile phone, I had promised myself solemnly that I wouldn't be one of those types who blithely use it while driving; one hand on the steering wheel and concentration all over the shop.

I spoke to his secretary. Yes, she had passed my message on. No, Mr Pitt had not offered me an appointment time. No, he had not said anything about my suggestion of turning up at the courts. I checked with her which case he was on and which court it was being heard in.

With all I'd heard about Rashid Siddiq from Emma I wasn't sure whether I'd be taking a risk with my own safety if I pursued an interview with him. Given he was one of the eye-witnesses, possibly the only eye-witness if Sonia Siddiq hadn't been there, it really was part of the job to talk to him, but I'd been putting it off. I checked my notebook and rang the warehouse. 'Can I speak to Mr Siddiq, please.'

'I'll get him for you.' The young woman failed to check out who I was and that could only work in my favour.

'Hello?'

'Mr Siddiq? My name is Sal Kilkenny. I'm ringing about the case against Luke Wallace. I'd like to arrange to talk to you about what you saw the night Ahktar Khan died.'

'I don't have to talk to you.' And he hung up.

He was right, he had no obligation to see me but I was

angry at the snub. My cheeks burned. I was aware that I was a stone's throw from where the Siddiqs lived, if he wouldn't see me then I'd call on his wife, see what she had to say about the allegations against her.

The white Saab was parked outside as before. I banged the lion's-mouth knocker. Sonia answered the door with the chain on; at the sight of me, her face widened with dismay.

'What do you want?'

'I want to talk to you.'

'I've said everything I've got to say.'

'Except the truth.'

'What does that mean?'

'You arrived at Nirvana at ten o'clock. Had tickets in advance, did you?'

'Yes.'

'Which floor did you sit on?'

'I don't see what this has to do—'

'What did you wear? What was the music like? Did you watch the videos? Did you like the decor? Could you describe it?'

Silence. Her face stony.

'You had a clear recollection of seeing the murder but everything else is very vague. Were you taking drugs?'

'No!' Outrage.

'People do – a lot of people do at these events. It's part of the culture, really.'

'Well, I don't.'

'Did you see people taking drugs?'

She shrugged.

'You see, I don't think it's because you can't quite remember, I think you just don't have a clue. Because you weren't there.'

'Of course I was there,' she insisted.

'That's not what I've heard.'

'That's rubbish. I was there. Why would I lie about it?'

'I don't know. Perhaps you were told to.'

'Who said this?'

'No one saw you there.'

'Zeb,' she said. 'He saw us. You ask him – Ahktar Khan's cousin, Zeb Khan.'

'I will. We can check easily enough anyway. They'd have you on tape, wouldn't they, coming into the club, those cameras? We could even confirm the exact time. Prove it one way or another.' I was bluffing. I'd no idea whether they did continuously record the club entrance, though I thought it likely. But how long would they keep the tapes before re-using them? She was completely still, her face blank, every ounce of energy going into hiding her reaction to what I'd just said. I had her scared witless. At last she spoke, her voice bright with bravado. 'Fine, you do that.' She shut the door.

Driving away from the courtyard I felt I'd gathered even more to relate to Dermott Pitt; much of it was intuitive rather than concrete, but my meeting with Mrs Siddiq had confirmed for me that she hadn't been present on New Year's Eve, and that her testimony was invented for someone else's benefit.

It was three thirty. I'd no need to collect Maddie and Tom; Ray did the school run on Mondays as he'd no lectures. I parked in the multi-storey car park near the college on Lower Hardman Street, and had to go up eight floors before I found a space. Then I cut through to Crown Square where all the Law Courts are.

Dermott Pitt would be in the Crown Court. I passed through a security arch where my bag was checked. At reception I asked for Court No. 2, and learned to my disappointment that they'd adjourned for the day. I walked down there anyway just in case Dermott was still hanging around chewing the fat with his colleagues.

The place was light and airy, with a long corridor, marble floors and pillars, and full-length windows all down one side giving a view of the square outside. On the other side were the courtrooms. At intervals there were statues of kings and lawgivers, and up on the wall opposite the windows, a huge colourful coat of arms, done in relief and surrounded by several smaller ones. My trainers squeaked on the floor; there was no other noise. The place was deserted. I poked my head into Court No. 2. There was an usher there who told me that they'd all left. 'He wanted to start fresh tomorrow with the defence witnesses.' She was referring to the judge.

'When do they break for lunch?'

'It's usually midday. He likes an early lunch, gets a bit rattled if they go on till one.'

'I'm trying to see one of the briefs, a Mr Pitt, about another case.'

'Ooh,' she pursed her lips, 'I wouldn't do lunchtime, they've often got a lot on then, depending on how the morning's gone. Need to see their clients and check the witnesses are all ready.' She shook her head. 'You'd be best coming at the end of the day.'

I nodded. Except the day might end early, like today. I tried Pitt's office on my mobile but they were engaged. I was reluctant to leave it at that. Bootle Street, the main city police station, was just across Deansgate. I'd call there – maybe they could get things moving.

Trying to report something – anything – to the police is always a hit and miss affair. It depends on the day, the desk sergeant, the weather, the football results, the position of the planets. The response can range from super-efficient: 'We'll have someone there within the next ten minutes, madam,' to the lackadaisical, 'You could try ringing Collyhurst/Copson Street/St Petersburg, next week, next year, next millennium, if you still want to report it. There should be someone there on a Thursday morning but we've a lot off sick today and it's not really our area.'

It helps if you know who you want to speak to, and which station they are based at.

Dermott Pitt would be more familiar with who to approach and what to tell them, but in his absence I wanted to do something tangible for Luke.

At the desk I asked to talk to someone from the Serious Crimes section. Before I got any further I had to give my name, address and date of birth. I then explained that I had new information that could materially affect the charges against Luke Wallace, on remand for murder. The desk sergeant took it all down and then disappeared through a door.

I waited. Read a wall full of Crime Prevention posters and Wanted posters and waited some more. When he returned he asked me to go with him. We went through the door and into a small room immediately to the left. An interview room? I waited a few more minutes then I was joined by a Detective Sergeant Hatton. He wasn't familiar with the details of the case so I did a quick resumé and then explained what I'd found out. Namely that the murder weapon belonged to one of the friends who had run away from home and was in hiding, and that there were inconsistencies in the statements given by the witnesses and even a question as to whether one of them had actually been present.

'Based on?'

'Well, hearsay at present, but I'm sure it could be proved.'

He grunted and rubbed his close-cut beard. Had I informed the brief for the defence?

'Not yet.' Trying hard.

He suggested I did so. The brief could then apply through the appropriate channels for the case to be reviewed. 'Sounds as though there may be some grounds there, the knife particularly, but they may decide to go ahead with the trial and debate the issues in full court anyway.'

And leave Luke on remand?

'We could have you in, take a full statement, go through

137

it all with you, but it wouldn't guarantee a result any quicker than using the legals. That's your best bet.'

No riding out on a white horse to rescue Luke from Golborne tonight then. I was disappointed. I'd been hoping for more decisive and compassionate action.

I had left a message at Rebecca Henderson's office on the Friday afternoon after my antics with Debbie Gosport. I wanted to cover my back so I made sure that the firm knew what had transpired, understood how badly Debbie's health was being affected and what advice I'd given her and her brother. I also informed Rebecca that the harassment now included assault, which would be significant in bringing any court action against G.

I was narked that I hadn't stuck with the stalker; he'd have received his papers by now if I had, but at the time I'd been convinced that Debbie's need was paramount.

Ricky rang late on Monday afternoon to let me know that Debbie and the children were staying with a friend in Chorlton. More letters had come to the house and he had intercepted them. Did I want to see them? Not particularly, but I asked him to hold onto them for evidence. The doctor had seen Debbie and changed her medication.

'Is it helping?'

'She's half-asleep,' he said, 'but at least she's not wired up like she was. She was up all night after you went, rabbiting on. Doin' my head in an' all.'

'I'm glad she's out of there, and that someone's with her.'

'Don't know how long she'll stay,' he said. 'She likes her own place, everything just so – you seen it.'

'Yeah. Ricky, there's a chance that the stalker will find out where she is and follow her again. Don't frighten Debbie, but tell her friend to keep an eye out and ring me if there's any sign. Make sure she's got my number.'

'She has. But how would he do that, find out where she is?'

'Not difficult. Wait at school, see where she goes . . .'

An intake of breath. 'Bastard.'

'It might not happen. Next time he surfaces I'll follow him home.'

'Next time,' he sneered.

I kept my voice even. 'Ricky, I've not done it yet but that's not because I'm no good at my job and it's not because he's particularly clever. It's just been a run of unfortunate circumstances.' And your sister's vanishing act hadn't exactly helped.

He grunted. Not convinced.

I didn't waste any more breath.

The day had been exhausting and little fragments from my meeting with Luke, my encounter with Mrs Siddiq and my visit to the police kept floating into my mind. I didn't want to be thinking about work. After tea I got a big map of Wales out and some old camping guides. I showed Maddie some of the places we could go.

'We haven't even got a tent, Mummy,' she said scornfully.

'We can borrow one. Harry and Bev have got one.'

'Ring them now, ask if we can.'

'Of course,' said Harry, to my delight, 'we're not using it.'

'Given up the outdoor life?' I joked.

'No, just prefer the warmer climes.'

I tutted. 'All right for those who can afford it.'

Harry and Bev had struggled financially for years, both working part time so they could share raising their two boys. Then Harry had got bitten by the investigative journalist bug, which meant long hours and not much more money. He'd begun to use computers as a tool for accessing commercial and business information; then he discovered the Internet and never looked back. Bev meanwhile had an unexpected pregnancy, and a third son came along. She never went back to her job and Harry began to rake it in, helping businesses get on the Net.

Sometimes they still seemed bemused by the radical change in their circumstances and their bank balance.

'Where are you going?' I asked. 'You're bound to let it slip when I'm least expecting it.'

'Saint Lucia, for three weeks.'

I groaned. 'So, the tent?'

'I'll ferret it out and all its bits for you, and drop them over some time next week.'

'Thanks.'

Maddie was delighted. Though, worryingly for me, her view of what we were heading for was coloured by roman-tic notions from her books and videos.

'We can catch fish, Mummy,' she said enthusiastically, 'and make a fire and cook them.'

'We'll see.' The classic get-out.

CHAPTER TWENTY

Tuesday. I hadn't had a swim for a week so went along to the early bird session as Ray could take the children to school. It was crowded and I couldn't build up the pace I wanted because I had to do so much dodging and weaving to avoid kicking someone in the groin or getting raked by a full set of toenails.

They cleared the pool, just before nine, ready for the schools to use. I could hear the whine of a drill and someone whistling. They were having some building work done at the baths, taking down an old outhouse at the back and strengthening the roof and back wall. The drill stopped and silence descended. In my cubicle I took off my goggles and got out my towel.

Boom! The vibrations of the almighty thump that followed the explosion went right through me. I put my arms up to shelter my head, using my towel for extra protection. *Not here, not now*, I prayed. *They can't bomb here!* My neck burned, there were spasms in my stomach. I held my breath and waited for the fallout, shivering, clammy with chlorine and sweat which prickled my armpits and broke onto my arms and sides. I was literally frozen with fear.

It was maybe a minute before intellect kicked in. No screams, no alarms, no bomb. *Stupid, stupid, stupid.* Demolition, not a bomb. Relief brought a new wave of sweat and shivering, I found my shower gel and walked unsteadily to the shower. My knees felt weak. I lathered and rinsed, lathered and rinsed, rubbing my legs, arms, stomach and shoulders vigorously, trying to take the gooseflesh away. By the time I was dressed, a crocodile of children were already filing into the place, chattering away, excitement breaking like bubbles and echoing round the room.

Diane was in the veg shop. Timing. 'Come back for coffee?'

She opened her mouth to say no but I interrupted. 'Please, there's something I need to talk to you about, and I really don't want to wait till tomorrow.' We were going for a drink the following evening.

'OK.'

She had to call at the Health Food shop on the way and I watched while she bought dried fruit, balsamic vinegar, apricot nectar and glycerine soap and geranium essential oil.

'Money?' I remarked.

'Just got paid,' grinned. 'The Corkscrews.'

The Corkscrews was her name for a series of prints she'd done in metallic colours with Mediterranean blue and burnt orange for a swanky new tapas bar in town. There were lots of spirals in them, hence the nickname. The bar liked them so much they were using her design as a logo for the menu and were having a wrought-iron and neon version done for the frontage.

At home I made coffee and we sat at the kitchen table. Digger muscled in on Diane who gave him a tickle behind the ear as she waited for me to explain.

I told her about my experience at the baths. She let me get to the end and then waited a while before commenting. 'It must be happening to lots of people. A sudden noise, flashbacks.'

'But I was nowhere near it. I was up the other end of Market Street, up near Piccadilly.'

'Near enough,' she retorted. 'You were there, you were

142

in town, you heard it – probably felt it, didn't you? It was strong enough to shake my windows.'

I nodded. 'You don't think I'm going mad then?'

She smiled. 'Do you?'

'No. It shook me up though. It was so unexpected, this instant reaction. So strong.'

'It makes sense, Sal. Don't beat yourself up about it.'

'Least I didn't run out into the street in my cossie or do anything else horribly embarrassing.'

'It's not happened before?'

'No. That's why it was such a surprise. God, I hope it doesn't happen again. What if it starts happening all the time?'

Diane laughed. 'That's it, think positive. Look – suppose it does, then you go and see someone, get help. There's counsellors and all that. But it's probably a one-off.'

I nodded. 'It was just that sensation. It was so . . . oh, I can't even explain it.'

By the time Diane left I felt I'd recovered enough to get on with my day. Just voicing my fears took the teeth out of them.

I made myself a sandwich and got some milk then walked round to my office. The Dobsons were out. There was only one piece of mail for me on the hall table. It was from the bank, who were trying to sell me a pension. Like something lurking to get me. Or not lurking actually. My erratic, often pathetic income puts me well out of the private pension league. The last time I read a breakdown of figures and returns in the paper I worked out I'd have to stop paying the rent or stop eating in order to pay contributions. No contest.

Downstairs there were no messages on the answerphone. I opened the window to air the room a bit, stuck the kettle on and made a list of the calls I wanted to make.

I'd been advised against trying to collar Dermott Pitt at lunchtime so I'd have to try and get in late afternoon, the worst time for me as I'd have to sort something out for the children. I couldn't do it today anyway, as Maddie had a friend coming for tea. Tomorrow then. I rang Dermott Pitt's office and asked his secretary to make sure Mr Pitt knew I would be waiting to see him tomorrow when the court finished its business for the day – say at four o'clock. I would go to his office if they had already adjourned.

'I don't know whether Mr Pitt will be free then,' she began.

'He'd better be,' I said, 'I've already been to the police and I'm sure he will want to know all the details so that he can represent his client properly.'

She hesitated, uncertain whether this was a threat or an insult. I carried on. 'I'll be there as I say, and if I'm not able to speak to Mr Pitt then I would feel duty bound to inform his client of his unavailability.' Duty bound? Why did I end up speaking their language?

Mr Wallace caught me before I'd made my coffee and demanded to know what was happening. He went ballistic when I explained that there'd been a delay in seeing Pitt and threatened to get onto it himself. I emphasized that I had a firm appointment fixed for the following afternoon and that I had been to the police. I managed to fudge the issue of why I couldn't ambush Pitt today instead of tomorrow by talking crisply about other work and pointing out that he wasn't my only client.

'I'm sure Pitt will give me a full hearing tomorrow and things will start to move,' I promised.

'What about this hypnotist?'

'Hypnotherapist.' Eleanor insists on the distinction. She doesn't want to be lumped alongside stage shows in which people do daft things in front of an audience. 'I'm going to ring her soon; she should be back from Golborne by now. I'll let you know how it went as soon as I have the details.'

The authorities had agreed to Eleanor using one of the

private consulting rooms at the Remand Centre for her session with Luke. 'It'll be much better if he can relax,' she had said, 'and the surroundings can help that a lot.' Eleanor was a friend of a friend who had given up working for Manchester Housing to retrain as a hypnotherapist. Her skills were used for all sorts: helping people to stop smoking, treating insomnia, teaching women to use hypnosis to ease the pain of childbirth. I had spoken to her, once the appointment had been fixed, to brief her on the background to the Wallace case; I covered the known and alleged events, and explained who the various people were and what the crucial time frame was.

When I rang her to see how the hypnosis had gone, she had just got back.

'You beat me to it,' she said.

'What happened? Did he remember anything?'

'No, I'm sorry, Sal. He remembers being in the club dancing and the next thing he's coming round at the police station. The rest is blank.'

'Nothing?' I was disappointed.

'Nothing.'

'You said he might be deliberately blocking things out, memories that he couldn't face.'

'Yes, but I don't think that's happening with Luke. If it was, I would have expected some restlessness, signs of unease when I asked him about that part of the evening but he was quite calm. He only became agitated as we moved on to the time when he was at the police station.'

And that would make sense if he'd been completely out of it beforehand. He comes to, in a cell, blood on his clothes and instead of tea and sympathy he gets unsmiling faces and cold, precise, repetitive questions to answer. The nightmare beginning.

'It makes it unlikely that he killed Ahktar then, doesn't it?' I asked her.

'I'm no specialist on criminals . . .' she began.

145

'I know, but in your opinion, if he had done it, you'd have expected a different reaction?'

'Yes, unless he had actually been in some sort of fugue state or was psychopathic and so lacked the appropriate emotional responses. Of course, the drugs confuse the issue.'

I sighed. 'Look, I know you've got to tread cautiously . . .'

'It's not an exact science.'

'But what's your opinion?' I insisted.

She laughed. 'OK, Sal. I'd be very surprised if Luke had killed his friend, and there's nothing to suggest he was even present when the attack took place.' It was confirmation of what I believed. I was glad of that – after all, it could have been disastrous if the session had revealed Luke as liable for the crime, but still I felt frustrated. We had not a shred more evidence about what had really happened that New Year's Eve.

I asked Eleanor if anything else had come up that I should know about.

'Let me check my notes. I tape the session but I jot down key words as we go – it helps in finding things on the tape.' A pause. 'Oh, yes. I asked about the other friends like you said, and I asked about any trouble. Now he mentioned Emma, the girlfriend, leaving and then Zeb, the boyfriend, had some sort of run-in with Joey. That's right – I asked him if it was a fight but he said it was just Zeb throwing his weight around.'

'Did he say whether he and Ahktar had fallen out?'

'Denied it, found it amusing so I don't think he was covering up.'

'And could you tell when the memory loss began?'

'Hard to be precise but definitely while he was still inside, before the end of the celebrations.'

'None of the others passed out,' I said, 'and they were all doing drugs.'

'Luke was drinking quite a lot too,' she replied. 'Extra-strong lagers.'

'Yuk.'

I recalled my own teenage experiments with that sort of drink. Strong enough to strip paint and intoxicating enough to have me senseless after two or three and hanging over the toilet bowl. Bad news anyway, but combined with a cocktail of drugs . . .'

'How was he?' I asked. 'I realize you have to keep things confidential, but . . .'

'That's OK. Luke and I discussed who I might talk to and what I would and wouldn't divulge. He's depressed and I've encouraged him to see the doctor there again. He's also experiencing periods of anxiety. It's not surprising, given the strain he's been under. I've offered to do some more hypnotherapy which could help reduce the stress and give him some techniques to manage the anxiety. He's keen so I'm going to have a word with his father about it later.'

'Good.'

I thanked Eleanor for her time. I'd be paying her for this first visit to Luke; it was warranted as part of my investigation. Of course, it would appear on Mr Wallace's next invoice as one of my expenses. I sorted out with her where to send her cheque and made a note for my own reference of the rate she charged. Just in case, I thought. If I had any more wobblers like the one at the baths that morning, I could consider a few sessions with Eleanor. I liked the notion of learning a bit of self-hypnosis. Could come in handy for lots of things, not just panic attacks. Those nights when the dog down the road keeps me awake, or moments when Maddie and I get locked into a spiral of argument and defiance.

'And obviously,' she said, 'the sooner this can be resolved, trial or release, the better for him. He's quite ill already and Golborne is no place to try and get better.'

So it was up to me, wasn't it? To find enough to force them to release Luke. Sooner rather than later. Me – and his lawyer.

CHAPTER TWENTY-ONE

When the bell went at the front door I waited to see if it would go again. I rarely got cold callers; most people ring and make an appointment. And any friend of the Dobsons would know not to drop in during a weekday. It rang again. I suspected it would be a doorstep seller, offering a great deal on tarmac, potatoes, lawn strimming or the latest fashion catalogue.

But it was Zeb Khan, a look of bravado on his face. My first reaction was to keep him out of the house. I hadn't forgotten the edge of aggression he'd shown me.

'Hello, Mr Khan.'

He glanced beyond me into the hall, back at my face. No, I wasn't going to invite him in. 'Can I help?'

'About Ahktar,' he spoke urgently, 'I've been thinking about it. It's not right, what you're doing. Wallace killed him. You just want to whitewash it all.' As he gained momentum he began to jab his finger at me.

'The court will decide who's guilty;' I said, 'and what evidence can be relied upon.'

'What's that supposed to mean?' he demanded.

'You saw Luke and Ahktar arguing but no one else did. Strange, that – such good mates, too. You'd think other people would have clocked it, if it had happened. And what about your row with Joey D? What was all that about?'

He glared at me. 'I don't know what you're on about.'

'You were shouting at him, grabbed him by the collar.

148

Can't you remember? Were you so smashed that you don't recall it? You owe a lot of money, don't you? Was it to do with that?'

He set his jaw. 'You should keep your fucking nose out, see, or you might get hurt. My cousin's dead.'

'Don't threaten me,' I said so he could just hear me. 'You threaten me and I might have to report you.' I locked onto his eyes. No way was he going to see me cowed. 'They'd be interested in that, wouldn't they? A witness nobbling one of the defence investigators. Worth looking into?'

He struggled briefly to contain his anger, lips pressed tight, jaw working away. Then he lost it. 'You cunt, you fucking—'

I shut the door quickly. Leant back against the wall for a moment, heart kicking at my stomach. *The knife-tip at my throat, needing to swallow, spittle on his lips* . . . I concentrated on my breathing. Felt my pulse begin to slow. I looked out through the spy-hole. Saw him kicking the gate open, leaving, thank God.

I was interested in the timing. I'd spoken to Mrs Siddiq the previous afternoon and now here was Zeb Khan warning me off. Must be getting too close for comfort. More evidence for Mr Pitt in the brief.

When I left to collect the children I felt edgy. I doubted that Zeb would actually attack me, he seemed more likely to do that in the heat of the moment, but being threatened had made me wary. I had a good look round before I left the Dobsons' and kept scanning the area on my way to school.

It was a long, slow walk back home, with a stop to buy a lolly for Tom and Maddie and Maddie's friend, Holly, and a second emergency stop when Maddie tripped and skinned her knees. She would die, she couldn't walk, all her blood was coming out. I've grown used to Maddie's low pain threshold and incipient hypochondria. I soothed until I'd had enough, then adopted a brisk, no-nonsense tone to steer her home.

There was a red car parked outside our house. A Mondeo. My heart squeezed hard. There was a man in the car. I shepherded the children up the drive. I heard the car door open and close. As I got them inside I turned to see who it was. I didn't know him.

He came up the drive. 'Miss Kilkenny?'

Ms actually, but now wasn't the time. I didn't commit myself 'What's it about?'

'Mike Courtney – freelance journalist.' He stuck out a large hand. I caught a whiff of spicy cologne. 'I believe you were the mystery woman at the Belle Vue suicide scene?'

The drone of flies, that putrid stench. Oh, hell. And he'd tracked me down – a dogged reporter. All I needed. 'There was no mystery,' I said coolly. 'The police have all the details.'

'Why were you calling on Mr Kearsley?'

'Kearsal.'

'Kearsal. Was it in connection with a case?'

'My work is confidential. There isn't a story, there's no mystery, you're wasting your time.' I tried not to snap. After all, I didn't want *MYSTERY WOMAN'S VOW OF SILENCE* or *SECRET SLEUTH WHO DARES NOT SPEAK* plastered all over the paper.

'There's a lot of interest in private eyes,' he pressed on. 'Look at the telly; Morse, Dalziel and Pascoe, The Bill.'

'They're police,' I quibbled.

'Well,' he shrugged, 'same difference. Readers may well be interested in a feature about your work. Woman in a Man's World, Girl Gumshoe – that sort of thing.'

Spare me. I'd have walked away then but I was all too aware of the need to build on my reputation, keep a steady flow of work coming in. If the piece was pitched right, it could be free publicity. 'Can I think about it?'

He looked impatient.

'I couldn't do anything now,' I explained, 'I'm in the middle of a job and I wouldn't want any publicity at the moment.' Like the stalker having my picture to alert him. 'I'm not sure about photos anyway. It could be a liability, if I was recognized.'

He sighed. This was going to be hard work.

'Sal!' Tom's voice called from inside, 'Sal!'

'Coming,' I replied.

'What about Mr Kearsal?' Mike Courtney persevered, 'They've not had the inquest yet. Will you be a witness?'

'I don't know. I've already explained the case was confidential.'

'The guy's dead,' he pointed out.

So it's OK then? To gossip and speculate and use him for a filler in the paper? The little house in the middle of an urban wasteland, the robbery that had made him fearful, escape to his sister's in Ashton now and then. 'Yeah, so let him rest in peace, eh?'

He tutted at me reproachfully then drew out his card. 'So you do all right for yourself?' He nodded up at the house. 'Make a decent whack or are you married?'

Oh, per-lease! 'No,' I lied, 'it's all mine.' Childish, I know, but he brought that side of me to the fore. And I enjoyed his envy. I marked him out as the type who can spend a whole evening talking about money, everything in Ks, only able to value what had a large price tag on it. I gave him an insincere smile and a goodbye and went in.

Maddie refused to let me touch the grazes on her knees, so I gave her a little lecture about hygiene and healing, and provided her with cotton wool, boiled water and some clean cotton cloths and strips of sticky plaster.

'I think Holly and you can sort something out,' I said. Holly was looking pretty brassed off by now with all the drama and no fun in sight. 'And if you clear it up I could put some water in the paddling pool.'

'My knees will get wet,' Maddie was appalled.

'Not if you just paddle,' I said firmly. 'And we can have a picnic for tea.'

'You could be the ambulance,' Maddie said tentatively to her friend.

'Paramedic,' Holly corrected.

I left them to it.

I made a pot of Darjeeling for myself and drank it with lemon, out on the patio. A ritual to settle myself. The weather had picked up – blue sky, a fresh breeze, puffy clouds moving fast.

There was so much to do. I emptied the disgusting contents of my slug traps and filled the pots with beer again. Despite the constant supply of fatalities they commanded I still lost countless plants. Half the petunias I'd grown from seed had gone, here and there a single central stalk, sheared to a point and smeared with silver, bore witness. They'd decimated the lobelia too. I reorganized the tubs, putting the survivors together.

The clematis needed tying in again. When I'd done that I got the shears out and went round to the front. The privet there was well out of control. It's one of my least favourite jobs, but it was beginning to interfere with free passage along the pavement. I chopped at it until it was a decent length, then brushed up the cuttings and stuffed them in the wheelie bin. I felt filthy by the time I'd done, covered in dust and spiders' webs and insects, my nails full of soil, throat parched, arms aching. On the plus side I no longer felt rattled by the turn that I'd had at the baths or by the unpleasantness of Zeb's visit. Working in the garden, the physical graft, the pungent smell and the feel of the earth had grounded me again.

'It's for you, Sal,' Ray called me to the phone.

I muttered my resentment. I'd just sat down to watch some telly.

'Hello?'

'Is that Sal Kilkenny?' Mrs Deason.

'Speaking.'

'Joey wants to meet you. He's given me the details. You won't tell the police?' She sounded desperate with worry. 'I promised to make sure you would go on your own, that you wouldn't bring anyone else. You won't try to trap him, will you? Nor force him to come back? I can't give you the details until I have your word.'

'I promise. All I want is to hear what Joey has to say.'

'He said to make sure you're not followed.'

'I will.'

A pause during which she must have checked that she'd asked all the salient questions. It stretched on.

'Mrs Deason?'

'He sounded dreadful,' she said abruptly, 'if only he'd just come home.' Her voice broke. 'When you see him,' she faltered, 'will you tell him that whatever happens he's still my grandson. I'll always . . .' she didn't need to finish.

'I'll tell him. Where have I to meet him?'

'He's not staying there,' she rushed to explain, 'you couldn't find him afterwards.'

'OK.'

'It's Prestatyn, in Wales. You're to meet at the railway station, twelve o'clock, midday.' High Noon in Prestatyn: Joey's liking for the dramatic. I knew the Welsh seaside town; I'd been to Prestatyn years ago. Remembered sitting on the concrete steps by the promenade waiting for the tide to give us back the beach. A long straight seafront, car parks, amusement place, couple of cafes. Its main attraction had been its proximity to Manchester; you could get there in a couple of hours. Not much else going for it apart from the sea, of course – ever-magical even in that setting.

'Thank you.'

'Will you let me know how he is?' She wasn't asking me to tell her what he'd said. If he had done it, she didn't want to know.

I promised. I was pretty sure I'd recognize Joey from

153

the photos I'd seen at her house so I didn't need to ask for a description.

I reckoned on two and a half hours to get there, allowing for hold-ups. It didn't matter if I was early but it would be disastrous if I was late. I'd be able to take the kids to school but I didn't know if I'd be back in time to pick them up. I asked Ray and he was able to rearrange his day so he could collect them.

Would I be back in time to see Mr Pitt at four, though? Possibly. I didn't want to ring and cancel now that I'd started putting pressure on him to see me. I would wait and see how the time played out, I decided. If I was delayed I could use my mobile and get a message to his secretary. Preserve my professional image.

I couldn't help speculating about Joey's reasons for agreeing to see me. To explain his innocence or defend his guilt? To protect his grandmother now that I'd uncovered her involvement in replacing the murder weapon? Was it a trap for me? My stomach lurched. Zeb had warned me off and that hadn't worked so now they were using Joey as a lure? No. I reassured myself. Joey was in hiding, not in cahoots with anyone. It was me who'd put the pressure on for a meeting. Was he hiding from Zeb? What had their argument been about?

I didn't sleep much that night. It was stuffy and I had the windows wide open. It felt as if the whole street was in my bedroom with me; the yappy dog, cars and taxis, a car alarm. When I did drop off my dreams were fretful. I was at school but I'd left Maddie at home. I got in the car but the steering wheel had gone. I was late; I was horribly late. I was so late that they'd all gone and left me. I was standing in the rubble and all the alarms were screaming but my legs wouldn't move. I reared awake and felt a wave of relief – just a dream. It was six o'clock. I lay there until the dream had faded then I started my day.

I was careful enough to leave details of where I was

going with Ray. I'd keep my mobile phone with me, and if anything seemed dodgy I'd get out of the situation as fast as possible. I hoped that I wouldn't get a call from Debbie Gosforth or her neighbours when I was halfway to Wales. Underneath my caution I was running with excited anticipation; things were on the move now. I had the buzz of making headway, the hunger to find out more. So I could finally make sense of the events of that fateful New Year's Eve.

CHAPTER TWENTY-TWO

After depositing the children at school I topped up the car with petrol and checked my oil, tyres and water. It was hardly a mammoth journey but I didn't want car trouble cocking it up.

It was a beautiful day for a trip to the seaside, sunny and still. The route into North Wales runs down around the outskirts of Chester, past Port Sunlight, home of soap and a host of chemical factories, and then along the coast.

There was an unmarked white transit van that had been a few cars behind me for some miles. Was I being followed? I watched it for the next few minutes. It was too far distant to see the occupants. Paranoia? After all, if the van was going to Rhyl or Llandudno this was the only route. Nevertheless I needed to set my mind at ease. There was a lay-by ahead with a Greasy Joe flying a Confederate flag. I pulled in and watched as the van passed me by. I got a glimpse of two people but couldn't tell anything more; it was going too fast. I sat for a while; the knot in my stomach gradually relaxed and then I drove on.

In the heat the farms and fields looked their best: luminous yellow rapeseed and green sugar beet stretching away to the distance, cows browsing. Now and then I caught the stench of fertilizer. I was sticking to the seat but I was only three miles from Prestatyn.

The resort was pretty much as I remembered it. I pulled into the car park next to the promenade. There was a large leisure centre to one side and behind me across a small road, a cafe and games room. I'd plenty of time to spare, as the station was only a few minutes' walk away. Good – I could fit in a paddle. I took my socks and shoes off in the car.

On the beach, the tide was out and the sand was still damp and hard-packed. My feet made little impression on its surface. I took a big breath of the briny smell and stretched my arms, then walked down to the sea's edge. The water was very cold. I dug my toes into the sand again and again, relishing the sensation, neither solid nor liquid.

There were a few families on the beach, though it was still term time, and a handful of individuals walking dogs. In a couple of months the place would be heaving, full of the ingredients of the great British seaside holiday: the smell of hot fat and vinegar and candy floss, shouts of children and sudden outbursts from harassed parents, rows of windbreaks and vacuum flasks, buckets and spades. And as often as not, rain or wind or jellyfish to round it all off.

I paddled along the shore for a while then made my way back up the beach looking for shells. There were a few cockles, small white and orange ones. The sand was littered with small dead crabs, pale green and brown, almost translucent. *Oh God – the flies . . . Mr Kearsal . . .* I shook the thoughts away and ran back to the car.

I made sure I was exactly on time. Joey D was waiting as he'd said by the ticket office. He wore a long-sleeved, outsize Adidas top and shiny black Adidas joggers. The baggy clothes seemed to emphasize his small frame. If I hadn't known better I'd have guessed he was thirteen or fourteen. He had short wavy blond hair and was very pale. Awfully pale – as though he'd been indoors all year or was malnourished. He wore black shades so I couldn't see his eyes. I introduced myself and he nodded, then looked around, beyond me. Was I being followed?

'I parked down at the beach and walked up here. Where do you want to go? Get a coffee?'

He shook his head. 'This way, there's some gardens.'

I didn't try to talk to Joey as we walked. I was busy assessing his mood. He was tense, twitchy and he kept coughing – a raw, painful sound.

We turned into a small formal park resplendent with municipal bedding plants; busy lizzies, brick-red geranium and silvery cinerama, its leaves like thick felt. There were benches around a bowling green, the grass smooth as peach skin. A party was playing, elderly men and women, joking with each other as they took their turns. The place felt tranquil and the atmosphere cheery. I wondered what they made of us; we were hardly here for the sport but no one paid any attention. How did he know this place? Had he been here before? I had a sudden image of Mrs Deason in full throttle playing for the away team, Joey on the sidelines. As if! I was sure he wasn't hiding in Prestatyn, but if he'd gone to ground in Liverpool or Warrington or Wigan he could have got here easily enough by train.

We sat side by side. He bit at his fingers, kept his face averted. Hard enough to read anyway behind his black glasses.

'Joey, you understand who I am and that I'm working for Luke Wallace's father?'

'Yeah.'

Now I'd got Joey D I didn't want to pussyfoot around. As far as I was concerned, the fact that he was here meant he'd talk to me, and I didn't want to have to drag it out syllable by syllable.

'Tell me what happened.'

'I'm not going back,' he said, 'I'm not going to be a witness – right? No police, no lawyers. Nothing.'

I felt a flash of anger at all his conditions.

'Why did you agree to see me, Joey?'

'I didn't do it – Ahktar,' he spoke rapidly. 'It was my knife but I didn't kill him. They could charge me, if you tell them about the knife. They'll think it's me then. They set Luke up, they can set me up too.'

'Hang on.' I rifled in my bag and brought out a small Dictaphone.

'Oh Christ.' He shook his head. 'No way.'

'Listen,' I made my voice hard, 'you telling me that you didn't do it is not enough. I need an account of what happened and I need it on the record. Especially if you intend to disappear later. If I go back with just your word and no proof to back it up, they'll be pulling your grandma in for questioning before the week's out. I need your statement. You say Luke was set up, I need proof. And if you haven't got the guts to come back and tell—'

'They'd kill me!' He became agitated.

I switched on the tape. 'Who'd kill you?'

'You don't get it, do you? They'd kill me. I go anywhere near Manchester, I'm dead.'

'Who? Why? Look – just tell me what happened,' I said gently.

He rocked back and forth on the bench a couple of times. Was he going to bolt?

Then he began to talk. 'We were coming out, been a good night, one of the best. All this energy, you know, no grief. Everyone's flying. Luke needed to throw up, he'd been mixing it, too much booze. We were gonna meet him outside, on the corner.'

We? Him and Ahktar? I didn't interrupt.

'There's these two guys, this big guy and another one. We're just going past them and one of them, the shorter one, grabs Ahktar from behind. He's got his arm up his back and he's holding his face so he can't turn round. At first I thought they were fooling around but then they hustled him into the alley. I'm going "Hey, hey, what are you doing, man? Get off him." They thump him in the guts and I get my knife out, right?' He swallowed, coughed violently and rubbed his hands on his thighs.

159

The sun was hot. I felt a bead of sweat trickle down my side.

'This guy turns and he moves so fast, he's twisting my arm, nearly breaks my wrist and I drop my knife.'

'Where's the other one?'

'Still got Ahktar, he's got his arms round his neck, holding him up. The one by me, the big one, gets the knife and . . . shit.' He squeaked the last word and fished in his pockets. Pulled out a packet of Benson & Hedges. It wasn't a cigarette he lit up but a small joint. Oh great, I thought. Now he gets busted for smoking dope before I get the full story. But no one blinked an eyelid. He dragged hard, sucking the smoke and holding it deep in his lungs. He erupted in a fit of coughing again.

'He's bending down, right?' His voice was tight. 'And he's just got the knife and Ahktar kicks out, kicks him in the face, hard. The guy rears up, he's screaming and . . . it happens so fast he sticks the knife in Ahktar. Then, I can't remember, it was all going off at once.' He took another toke, held it in, released a stream of smoke.

'What did Ahktar do?'

'He smiled,' there was a note of disbelief in Joey's voice. 'The guy lets go of him and starts jabbering on. Ahktar sits down.'

'What was he jabbering about?'

'I didn't get it all. Lot of it was Punjabi or whatever.'

'They were Asian?'

He nodded. 'But he was swearing, at his mate. "You fucking prat," he said, "we weren't supposed to do him, just a little warning. You stupid cunt, you stupid, stupid fucking cunt." He's really going mental. I shouted to them to get an ambulance and I called Ahktar. He's slumped over. I tried to get near but the guy that done it's between us. I'm calling, "Ahktar, Ahktar," and the guy stares at me. I say, "He needs an ambulance, he could die, man." He just stares at me, really freaky, then the little one starts screeching again, really losing it. "You done wrong," he's going, "you done wrong, man. What's he gonna do when he finds out?" On and on he goes till the big one tells him to fucking shut up. I could see all this blood soaking through Ahktar's jacket and I legged it. I wanted to get help. The big guy comes after me.' He shuddered and drew hard again on his joint. 'He pulled me back into the alley. He got me real close and said he'd find me. If I breathed a word he'd find me and he'd kill me. He asked me if I understood. I said yes. Then he got my hand. He twisted my finger back.' He rubbed his little finger, looking at it as he spoke. I could see it was slightly crooked. 'It snapped, he broke it.' Joey began to shake. 'He asked me again if I understood and I said yes. Christ, it fucking hurt. Then he broke the other one next to it. I was crying, right, and he slapped me. Told me to shut up. He said if he ever heard of me, any whisper about it, he'd find me and he would kill me very slowly, bit by bit.' Joey paused. 'I went home,' he said flatly, 'I rang an ambulance up on Oxford Road. Then I went home.'

I recalled Mrs Deason, the fleeting gesture she'd made with her hands, on the brink of telling me what they'd done to Joey's fingers.

'Did you go to hospital?'

'No. My gran, she strapped them up.'

I watched the bowlers for a while. The gentle banter as one player missed her stroke. Joey ground the roach out underfoot. Coughed some more.

'And Luke? When the ambulance arrived they found Luke with Ahktar. Unconscious.'

He shook his head. 'They set him up.'

I wondered how. Had Luke come looking for Ahktar and been given a timely blow to the head, or had they found him by chance, passed out perhaps. A suspect of convenience. They must have wrapped his hand around the knife to get the prints.

I asked Joey to describe the men. He did, and I quickly recognized the picture that he drew of the larger man, the one who had used the knife. Rashid Siddiq. Killer turned witness.

CHAPTER TWENTY-THREE

'I got to go.' He made a move.

'Hang on, I've a few more questions.'

'Christ,' he rocked with impatience. The dope didn't seem to have settled him any. He sniffed again. Summer cold or cocaine eating away his nostrils? Joey D was a mess.

'Why do you think they killed Ahktar?'

'It was an accident,' he said simply. 'They were meant to give him a warning about something, that was all. The guy just went ballistic when Ahktar kicked him.'

And if he hadn't had your knife, I thought, the blow wouldn't have been fatal.

'If you talked to the police,' I began.

'No way.' He went rigid. 'I already said, no police, no lawyers, nothing.'

'You could get protection,' I said.

'Oh yeah?' he said sarcastically. 'Twenty-four-hour guard, safe house, you reckon? All that for me? No way.'

'What would they want to warn Ahktar about?'

'Search me.' He twitched again, an involuntary movement as though his skin were alive. 'Look, I got to go.'

'I've nearly finished. You hadn't heard anything about Ahktar getting involved in anything?'

'Dodgy? No. Bit of a nerd really, Ahktar. Nice guy but he wanted to be a lawyer, lot of studying. He partied at weekends, getting happy with the rest of us but that's all.'

Secretly, I agreed. His recreational drug use was not

reason enough for the heavies to come along and threaten him.

'Do you remember Zeb having a go at you that night, in the club?'

'Yeah.' He was puzzled by my interest.

'What was that about?'

'He wanted a loan – he owed a lot of money. He was trying it on, promised to pay me ten per cent interest. I have this trust fund,' he explained. 'I told him no way, might as well flush it down the bog, never see it again. So he tries getting all heavy, threatening me, says he'll put me out of business. I laughed at him. I'm only getting stuff for friends, I'm not a dealer, for chrissakes.'

'Did you ever get stuff from Zeb?'

'Once, maybe twice. And a couple of times he gets some from me. Dunno why, he could get more than I ever saw. Reckon he'd been helping himself, got a bit greedy, needed to top the bag up. He'd be paying over the odds getting it from me – last in the chain you get the highest mark-up. No head for business.' Joey was serious. We could have been talking about building society flotations.

'I've heard he was involved in bringing drugs into the country. Did you know about that?'

He shrugged. 'You hear stuff; I didn't want to know. That's way out of my league. I never got into all that, I'm strictly small time.' He grinned and for a fleeting moment he was a teenager having fun walking on the wild side. He coughed again.

'Did you ever meet Rashid Siddiq? He worked with Zeb and his brother Jay?'

He shook his head.

'How did you get the knife into the club?'

'Gerry, one of the bouncers, he's a customer of mine. I slip him a bit of something to help him relax at the end of the night, we had an understanding.' He bit on his fingers again, tearing slowly at the skin around his nails.

'How are you?' I asked him. 'Your grandmother's worr—'

'Sound,' he cut me off. Sniffed.

'You doing a lot of drugs?'

'You a social worker in your spare time?'

'You look rough, Joey. You look ill.'

'Fuck off.' But he didn't move.

I watched the next couple of strokes.

'It's hard to get hold of stuff sometimes, that's all. I get a bit shaky. Start crashing, you know. Stressed out, start to see things that aren't there.' He twitched. 'Think people are following you. Does my head in. I just need a steady supply, that's all. Get that sorted, no problem. I can handle it.' He was all bravado now. 'Tell her I'm OK.'

'You still in business?'

He burst out laughing. 'Yeah. You think I'm gonna start working at McDonald's or something? Go on some pissy training scheme?'

A bee, heavy with pollen, careered towards us and bumped into Joey's cheek. He swatted at it with his hand and knocked his shades off. The sunlight made him wince and he shielded his eyes with one hand while he searched for his glasses with the other. I got them first and handed them to him. His eyes were bloodshot, streaked with red capillaries, watering in the sudden light. Was that drugs too? Or illness or lack of sleep?

My guess was that it was all bound up together. The drugs that once gave Joey pleasure, not to mention profit, now brought paranoia and pain. He was an addict like his father before him, out of control.

'I got to go.' He stood up, trembling a little.

I clicked the tape recorder off. 'Another appointment?'

'Need to see if anything's arrived yet, stuff's been in short supply this last couple of days.' No wonder he was so twitchy.

'If you change your mind about . . .'

'I won't,' he looked away from me.

'I can play them this tape but I don't know whether it's enough to get Luke off. They have witnesses who are prepared to testify, to appear and say Luke killed Ahktar. If you'd come to an identity parade?'

'No.'

'But—'

'It won't bring Ahktar back, will it? And they'll kill me.'

'How long are you going to hide?'

'Long as it takes.'

'And Luke?'

'I told you what went down. That's it. I got to go.' He walked away.

I watched him go, off to buy a bit more oblivion. I wondered what the drug culture would be like by the time Maddie was exploring it. How would I protect her from the worst excesses whilst letting her take the risks that all teenagers sought? Hah! I thought, I won't. I'll be on the sidelines worrying, trying not to let it show. If I can't even get her to talk to me now about what goes on at school, she's hardly going to confide in me about her drug taking!

A patter of applause at the end of the game and then the bowl-players were called for tea over at the small clapboard pavilion at the far side of the green.

I left the park and made my way back to the car, calling in at the public toilets below the entertainment complex. They were all galvanized steel and mottled concrete floors reeking of industrial-strength disinfectant and damp concrete, resilient to seawater, sand and the ravages of tourists.

I passed the train station on my way back to the main road but there was no sign of Joey. In the car park I noticed a white van. Unmarked. My stomach flipped and my heart stammered. I reasoned with myself all the way home, but the worry wouldn't go away. It just lodged there like a bone in my throat.

When I arrived back in Manchester I felt sticky from

the journey and my shoulder was stiff from the combination of driving and fretting, but I decided to strike while the iron was hot.

I was on time; it was nearly four o'clock, but the court was empty again. Finished for the day. No wonder the wheels of justice took such a long time to turn. I felt like kicking the statues in frustration. Instead, I rang Mr Pitt's office. My bullish tone the previous day must have had some effect because the secretary greeted me with something bordering on warmth and told me she was glad I'd got in touch; Mr Pitt had been called out at short notice on a matter of some urgency, but was very anxious to hear what I had to say. Could I leave a number where I could be reached this evening? I gave her my home number and my mobile – I was going for a drink with Diane. She had no idea when he might call and warned me it could be quite late. I reassured her that any time was fine.

I should have rung Mrs Deason, then. But I was putting it off. Still hoping that my fears about the white van were unfounded. What would I say? He's a wreck, Mrs D. He's all skin and bone, he's got a graveyard cough, he's jumpy as hell, nerves shot to pieces and when he's not got enough drugs he's getting panic attacks and paranoia. Oh, and by the way, I think I was followed to Prestatyn. They may be on his trail – the people who want to keep him quiet. The people who broke his fingers. So, I put it off, deciding to call her the next day. And in the meantime try and get things in perspective.

It was warm enough to sit outside the pub for the first hour. As it got darker the midges drove us inside. Diane had not tried any more lonely hearts' adverts.

'I haven't had time,' she said. 'I've been working flat out. You know, they did a feature on dating agencies on Richard and Judy.'

'Diane.' She knows daytime TV makes me squirm.

'It's very educational,' she remonstrated, 'popular culture. As an artiste,' she waggled her eyebrows, 'I feel obliged to keep up with the trends of the time. To have my finger on the pulse.'

'Be better off on the remote control,' I muttered.

She ignored me. 'They were saying how hard it is to meet new people these days. A lot of couples meet through work so that rules me out.'

'What about your commissions, your patrons or whatever?'

She snorted. 'Hah! No nice Spanish restaurateurs as yet. No, the place that wants the corkscrews is owned by a woman with a string of caravans in Southport and some boarding kennels in Hyde. Talk about diversification.' She took a swig of her drink.

'I've been to the seaside today,' I confessed. 'Work, not pleasure. Well, I had a paddle.'

'Southport?'

'Prestatyn.'

'I got stung by a jellyfish in Prestatyn,' she said. 'Awful. I could feel the poison travelling round my body for hours, honestly. Little stings and prickles breaking out everywhere, even my eyelids. Hardly a mark on me but bloody painful. So how was sunny Prestatyn?'

'Depressing.' I told her a bit about my meeting with Joey, about all the new evidence and the fishy bits, and how shaky the case now seemed against Luke. 'Though that's my impression. A lot of what I've got could be ignored. They might still want to go to trial, argue about it all there. I just wish it were sorted.' I told her about the white van. 'I think I might have been followed there. I'm worried about Joey, if they know he talked to me . . . Do I sound paranoid?'

'A bit. It's hardly surprising though, is it, what with the stalker thing and the fright you had yesterday. You sleep last night?'

'Not well.' I thought of Joey's blood-red eyes.

Eating?'

'Lots,' I smiled.

'OK.' She was all practical now. 'You're going to see the lawyer tomorrow?'

'Yeah – well, I'm hoping he'll ring me tonight. If he doesn't I'll sit in his court all day if I have to.'

'So, it'll soon be over,' she pointed out.

'Yes,' I said with more certainty than I felt, 'see the brief, do my final report for Mr Wallace, include my invoice and leave them to it.'

I was feeling mellow by the time we left and ready for a decent night's sleep. Our bikes were locked side by side at the back of the building. We'd released them, sorted out helmets and lights and said our farewells before wheeling round to the road. Parked on the opposite side was a plain white van. I felt dizzy. My mouth went dry.

'Diane – the van. I think it might be the same one.'

'Oh God.'

I noted the number plate. There was someone in the driver's seat. It looked like Rashid Siddiq but it was dark and I could only see a profile. Was it the same van? My intuition was telling me loud and clear to be scared, to be careful.

'Will you ride back with me? You could get a taxi home.'

'Come on.'

We mounted up and set off. The van remained at the kerbside. We rode the two miles or so to my house. There was no sign of the van.

Diane came in for a cup of tea and a post mortem. I wanted her to stay the night, anxious that she might be at risk because of me, but she was keen to go home.

'I'm irrelevant,' she insisted.

'Get a taxi then.'

'Sal!'

'Please, take your wheel off, get a black cab. I'll pay. Please.'

She sighed but agreed to my demands. I saw her off in the taxi and made her promise to ring when she got back. In the moments while I waited I imagined her being attacked as she reached her home. Over and over I ran the images. I should never have let her go. I'd once been beaten up practically outside her door. That had been a warning to me to keep my nose out of a case I was working on, too.

When the phone rang I snatched it up. She was fine. We said our goodbyes and she told me several times to take care. Not that I needed the advice.

I was too wired to sleep so I made more tea. I sat in the lounge cruising channels and watching four things at once. Digger lay beside me, peering at me now and again out of one sleepy eye. We don't have much time for each other, Digger and I, but the dog seems to have a sixth sense when I'm feeling bad and comes to give me some companionship.

The phone rang again. Dermott Pitt?

'Hello?'

'Sal Kilkenny?'

'Yes.'

'It's Mrs Raeburn.'

'Who?'

'Debbie's neighbour. He's back. You said to ring, and he's here now. The stalker.'

The perfect end to a perfect day.

CHAPTER TWENTY-FOUR

'He's across the road, just standing there. Debbie's still away but the lights are on. I said to Ricky, her brother, that I'd pop in now and then, open the curtains, put the lights on, make it look lived in.

'Thank you,' I stopped her carrying on, 'I'll be right over. I'm hoping to follow him home, so don't come out or do anything to alert him to the fact, will you?'

'No, no of course.'

As usual, when I have to work at night, I left details with Ray of where I was going. I felt an extra edge of caution, given the unwelcome presence of a suspicious white van in my life. There was no sign of it on my drive over to Chorlton, however much I checked and rechecked.

I drove along Debbie's road. G was still there – a slight, still figure in the shadows. I passed him and drove on looking for his blue Fiesta. I found it down the street; luckily there was a space a bit further on where I could park. I'd be facing in the same direction too, which would help when following him. I jotted down his registration number.

The house I parked outside looked to be a student let – several doorbells, grass in the guttering, a plaque with the name of the property management company over the door. It suited me. I was less likely to get quizzed by a member of the local Neighbourhood Watch if I sat waiting outside a house with plenty of tenants.

I reclined my seat and laid back; no point in flaunting

myself. My mobile rang, startling me. It was Dermott Pitt. He apologized for the lateness of the hour and said that he had received my message.

'I've got a tape I'd like you to hear, from Joey D – Joey Deason,' I told him. 'He actually saw the murder take place. His knife was used, taken from him when he tried to defend Ahktar. His grandmother replaced the knife after Joey had run away. He's described the killer and it sounds like Rashid Siddiq,' I paused for breath. Then:

'I've also got some information about the Siddiqs which would fit with Joey's version of events. I've spoken to someone at Bootle Street about some of this, before I saw Joey. They advised me to take it to you.'

'Eight o'clock?'

'Pardon?'

'I can do eight a.m. I'm in court from nine thirty.'

'Yes.' Even if I had to take the kids in with me. 'I'll be there.'

I felt a surge of relief after the call. Pitt was taking it seriously; it would soon be over.

I considered calling Mrs Deason but it was so late. I'd do it first chance I got in the morning, see if there was any way she could contact Joey and warn him about the white van.

I switched on the radio for company. It was very quiet now and most of the lights in the houses had gone out. Cats claimed the street, slipping under gates and over fences, stalking prey. I shifted in my seat; already my buttocks were getting numb and I wanted to wee.

How long would we be here? What did he do all the time, standing there? Was he thinking about Debbie? Did it excite him? Was that how he got his kicks? Why had he picked on Debbie for the focus of his obsession?

I was tired, my eyes felt gritty and my teeth felt furry, but there was no danger of me dozing off, I was far too uncomfortable. To occupy myself I rehearsed what I would tell Dermott Pitt when we met tomorrow. I'd start with the tape. Then explain how the knife had been replaced. I'd tell him about my suspicion that Sonia Siddiq had been pressed to be a witness for the prosecution, and my anonymous tip-off that she hadn't even been at the club. Describe her reactions to my questions, and point out that Zeb's story of the two lads arguing could have been invented to increase the plausibility of Luke being the killer. I'd put it to him that Zeb Khan and the Siddiqs had conspired to frame Luke Wallace for the murder of his best friend.

I was convinced. Admittedly, there were a few aspects that were still a mystery to me. I didn't know exactly how they'd engineered it so that Luke was found as he was. I didn't understand why they'd framed him, rather than lying low and leaving the police to try and figure out whodunit. After all, there were no witnesses apart from Joey, who had easily been silenced. And I still couldn't get my head round why Ahktar Khan had needed a warning in the first place, or who the warning was from. Jay employed Rashid Siddiq, so it was pretty likely to be his instruction that Siddiq and his accomplice were carrying out. But why? What had Ahktar done or not done? Had he found out about the drugs operation and threatened to tell? Tell who? Family? Police? If that had been the case, would he have seemed so comfortable and carefree that evening? The image of a whistle-blower didn't suit the impression I'd built up of Ahktar. Yes, he worked hard at his studies, but he was well-liked, popular. And not averse to dropping a tab or taking speed to get high with his mates.

I was trying to predict Mr Pitt's response when I saw the stalker, in my rear view mirror, returning to his car. It was one thirty. As he got into the Fiesta I righted my seat, rubbed my eyes and breathed deeply a few times to wake myself up.

I waited until he'd pulled out and reached the junction with the main road before following. I wasn't likely to lose him at that time of night unless he burned rubber. If he was paying any attention he would soon notice I was on his tail, but his mind was probably still occupied with his fantasies about Debbie Gosforth, and I reckon if people aren't expecting to be pursued they can drive for miles before the penny drops and they realize the car behind isn't going their way by chance.

We went along Upper Chorlton Road towards the city. The streets were mostly deserted though there were a couple in a clinch waiting for an all-night bus at the stop near the huge Whalley Hotel Pub. We stopped at the lights there. I yawned a couple of times but underneath my exhaustion there was a tremor of excitement building as I realized I was on course, trailing him back to his lair so I could establish his identity. We turned left into Ayres Road where he parked. I drove past him, reducing my speed to a crawl. I parked in the next side road, got out quickly and doubled back in time to see him open the door of one of the terrace houses and go in. Lights came on in the hall. I walked along to the house and noted the number.

The quiet in the street was interrupted by the clatter of a black cab coming from the main road. It drew up nearby and after a few seconds the back door swung open and two young women giggling hysterically fell out onto the pavement.

'Gerroff, yer divvy, yer breaking me arm.'

'You get off.'

'I can't move, you bloody great lump.'

One of them kicked the door shut with a large silver platform shoe. Amidst much cursing and cackling the pair disentangled themselves and stood up, more or less, on teetering heels. They'd been out on the razz and were still having fun.

The taxi pulled away. The silver platforms belonged to a woman in silver lycra boob-tube and shorts. She began to snigger again.

'Shut up, Jules,' her friend protested, 'I've already wet myself.'

'Ha ha ha ha.' It was infectious and I found myself smiling. 'Ha ha ha ha.'

'You got any fags left? Jules, got any fags?' She wore a black sheath dress and had glitter in her hair. 'Where's the bleeding key?' She rummaged around in a clutch bag.

'Some fags inside, Mel,' said Jules. 'Think there's some left.'

'There better be, I'm gagging.'

They turned and swayed towards the doorway of the house.

'Excuse me,' I said.

'Why, what yer done?' quipped Jules and the pair dissolved in giggles.

When the racket had died down a bit I carried on. 'Do you know the bloke next door but one?' I pointed.

'Which one?' asked Black Dress.

'Mr Upstairs or Mr Downstairs?' More snickers.

'Oh, I thought . . . there's only one bell.'

'Landlord's too bloody tight to give 'em a bell each.'

Her friend staggered and the two lurched towards me reeking of heavy-duty perfume and cigarette smoke.

'Is it flats then?' I asked the woman in black, who seemed less prone to hilarity.

She shrugged. 'Not really, there's only one bathroom but he sticks a Baby Belling on each floor and lets 'em out like flats. Same as ours.' Jules knocked her again and she dropped her bag. The contents scattered; lipstick, perfume and eye-pencil, cigarette lighter, tissues and purse, keys. I helped them gather everything up. 'Here's your key.'

'Ta. So, what do you want?'

'I need to find out the name of one of the people living there.'

'Why, you from the social?' Her eyes narrowed with suspicion.

'No, no,' I smiled. 'He helped me out. I just broke down,' I waved towards the main road, 'and he spent ages on my car, got it going again. I'd like to send a card or something, thank him.'

'Ooohh!' remarked Jules, lips pursed, all innuendo. I rolled my eyes at her. 'Do you know their names?'

'Gary, innit,' Jules volunteered, 'Gary Crowther and upstairs is Chris, whass Chris's name, Mel, something Irish innit?'

'Scottish, not Irish – McPherson.'

'I thought he was Irish.' Jules shook her head. 'I could've sworn he was Irish, innit.'

'He's a Geordie, yer div.'

'You just said he was Scottish.'

'His name! Scottish name. But he's from Newcastle.'

'Can you describe them?' I interrupted the debate. I kept looking over to the stalker's house, hoping that the commotion that Mel and Jules were making was a regular occurrence and wouldn't attract his attention.

'Gary's dark hair, Chris's brown, light brown.' Mel looked to Jules for confirmation.

'Yeah, Chris is the good-looking one.'

'He is not,' she contradicted, 'he's got small eyes. Gary's better-looking.'

'What about size?' I asked, regretting the words even as they left my lips.

'Size is not important,' cackled Jules.

Mel snorted with laughter but recovered quickly. 'Don't mind her,' she said, 'she's got a one-track mind.'

'You must be interested in him, aren't yer? Your knight of the road,' teased Jules.

'Shurrup.' Mel shoved her. ' 'Bout the same, they are. Medium height, medium weight.'

I needed something more definite. The man I'd followed had dark hair, almost black, but hair colour alone wasn't enough to confirm his identity:

'Does either of them wear a suit? The bloke who helped me wore a dark suit.'

'Gary,' they said in unison.

'Probably sleeps in it,' said Mel, 'had it for years, by the look of it, be back in fashion soon. I said to him the other day, "get some shorts on, kid, let yer knees out".'

'You know him then?'

'She is interested, innit,' commented Jules.

Mel elbowed her in the ribs. 'Don't know him well. Just neighbours, same bleeding landlord. He's shy, Gary. Wouldn't say boo to a goose. Goes red as beetroot every time I say hello.'

I smiled. 'Well, thanks for your help,' I said, 'goodnight then.'

'Will you get this door open,' complained Jules. 'I need a fag, innit.'

Once they'd gone in I looked back at Gary Crowther's house.

Gotcha! Name, address and number plate. I turned on my heel and walked briskly to my car.

I drove carefully home, aware of how tired I was and how easy it would be to make one fatal mistake. I was pleased I could now get things rolling on Gary Crowther, but the pleasure was muted by my overriding need to sleep.

CHAPTER TWENTY-FIVE

I'd had maybe two and a half hours when Maddie woke me, complaining of earache. I stumbled about sorting her out with Calpol and let her into my bed. She fretted and whined and wriggled about for ages before falling asleep. I hoped she'd be better by morning. I couldn't take time off to nurse her. I dozed for another hour and woke at half six and gave up on sleep.

Maddie was still in pain when she woke up at seven. It was too early to ring the GP. I had to be in town to meet Dermott Pitt at eight. I knew Ray would be leaving for work at eight so I had to find someone to take Tom into school and someone to mind Maddie till I'd had my meeting. I rang Nana 'Tello, Ray's mother, who sounded decidedly grumpy though she always claimed she couldn't sleep in the mornings. She agreed to look after Maddie for me. I called over the road to Denise, apologized for the short notice and asked if she could take Tom in with her daughter Jade. No problem. Ray would bring Tom across at eight.

There was no sign of the white van when Maddie and I set out. Nana 'Tello made a fuss of Maddie in a mixture of Italian and baby talk. Maddie was too wiped out to react to it. We settled her on the sofa. The telly was tuned to a sports channel. Nana 'Tello would be studying the form for the day's races. I promised to be back by ten.

'It's a shame,' Nana 'Tello said as she saw me out, 'when

you gotta go rushing off to big meetings and your little girl so poorly.' It was. But what could I do? I didn't draw support from the comment either. I'd heard enough of her views on motherhood and work to know that she wasn't sympathizing with my predicament. Thank God she didn't follow through on her beliefs and refuse to help out when the crunch came. I thanked her again and joined the rush-hour traffic into Manchester.

Queuing to get into the multi-storey car park made me five minutes late. Enough to have me running to the solicitor's offices and leave me out of breath on my arrival.

You'd never have guessed that Dermott Pitt had worked late last night and risen early in the morning. He looked fresh and neatly turned out when his secretary led me through.

'Coffee?' she asked him.

'Excellent. Ms Kilkenny?'

'Please.' Oh yes, please. The smell of it had made me dizzy when I'd walked in.

She must have had it waiting. She returned immediately with an exquisite pair of hand-painted coffee cups on a tray along with a cafetière, a jug of milk, a bowl of multi-coloured granulated sugar and plate of thin, dark chocolate biscuits. I was ravenous. I wanted a fluffy cheese and tomato omelette with wholemeal bread and butter, pancakes dripping with golden syrup and sprinkled with fresh lemon juice. Or a full English breakfast without the sausage and bacon. I don't eat meat but the rest would do very nicely. Eggs, mushrooms, tomatoes, fried bread, toast and marmalade. There were five biscuits. Who'd get the last one?

'I have until eight forty-five,' Dermott announced pompously, 'I am all ears.'

'I brought the tape. I think you ought to listen to that first.'

I handed him the cassette and he moved to open one

of the antique wooden cabinets to his side. It concealed a state-of-the art midi system. He put the tape in. I knew I'd successfully recorded Joey – I'd checked the end of the recording on my return from Prestatyn. In the past I'd once proudly played someone a cassette which proved their foreman was filching goods, only to find the tape was completely blank. Never again.

Dermott sat back and steepled his fingers. The tape began, birdsong and traffic sounds louder than I remembered. For a moment or two I was embarrassed at the sound of my own voice but it didn't take long to be drawn back into Joey's story of the killing.

Pitt indicated that I should help myself to coffee and I did. I inhaled the steam until it was cool enough to sip. Pitt poured his own and took a biscuit. I took a biscuit. Then another. Joey talked about Ahktar smiling, about calling out to him. The story unwound.

'That's it,' I said when the sound stopped. 'And the man he describes, the big bloke, I think that's Rashid Siddiq.'

'But he won't formally identify him,' he sighed.

'There's more,' I said, 'if I can . . .'

'Yes.' He made notes as I talked.

'There are doubts about whether Sonia Siddiq was even there that night. I had an anonymous phone call telling me she was making it all up. She became very uncooperative when I asked her to recall any details about the event or the venue. I'm sure she's lying. Someone, probably Rashid, has rehearsed her. It would also fit with the delay in them coming forward as witnesses; they couldn't do it immediately. I think they've discussed it all with Rangzeb Khan as well. He came to threaten me.'

Mr Pitt stopped writing and raised his eyebrows at me.

'It was the day after I'd challenged Sonia Siddiq. And Zeb has got this story about seeing the two lads arguing, which no one else saw, and everybody else I've spoken to thinks is laughable.'

'He threatened you?'

'Told me I was making a big mistake, that I was trying to whitewash it all. Mouthed off, got quite abusive. And since then I think I've been followed. This white van, they trailed me to Prestatyn – they might be after Joey D. And they followed me again last night.'

'Did they follow you here?'

'No – at least I didn't see anything.' Maybe they'd made their point and that would be the end of it. 'Will this get Luke out?'

'I can't promise anything but I'll be making an application for bail on the basis of what I've just heard. If the CPS have any sense they will look again at the case and discontinue; they may even refer it back to the police as it implicates someone else. Of course, they can hold on and fight it out at trial but I'd be surprised if Luke Wallace isn't bailed until then. I must admit I am concerned that Joey Deason is not prepared to make a formal identification. It would make our case significantly stronger, but . . .'

'There's no way,' I said, 'you heard him, he was adamant. But even if you can't prove that Siddiq was the one who stabbed Ahktar, you can show that it's very unlikely that Luke did. He had hypnotherapy, you know, and the therapist says there was nothing to suggest he was present at the scene; everything indicates that he was still in the club and out of his box when Ahktar was attacked.'

'Tricky area, hypnosis.' He leant forward and took his second biscuit. There was one left on the plate.

'Yes, but it fits with everything else.'

'And you think Luke was deliberately placed at the scene of the crime? Why? Why not just quit the scene?' He spoke irritably, as if it was my fault that all the pieces didn't fit. 'If he was incapacitated, what propelled him to that side alley – round the back of the building, out of sight? He wouldn't have known Ahktar Khan was there.'

He echoed my own queries.

181

'I don't know. Chance? If he stumbled upon them, it may have just seemed like a good idea at the time, to confuse the issue.' I couldn't bear it any longer. I grabbed the biscuit. 'Unless he was told. Or they found Luke practically comatose and put him there, hoping the police would jump to conclusions. Which they did. It worked. They find Luke covered in blood, his prints on the knife, unable to remember anything. Once Zeb comes forward with his report of the quarrel and the Siddiqs give a complete eye-witness account, then it's a cinch. Look no further.'

'It's possible. But Siddiq and the other assailant, they didn't know Luke Wallace, did they?'

'No, I don't think so. But Zeb did; he knew him as his cousin's best friend.'

'There's nothing on the tape to suggest Zeb Khan was present.'

'I don't think he was, not during the murder. But maybe after . . .' I was speculating. 'You're right,' I conceded. 'I don't know how Luke came to be there, or why. I bet they were panicking at the time. The murder was a mistake. For some reason they left Luke at the scene, or put him there, or he found his way there, but it was later they worked out that providing eye witnesses would stitch it up. Rashid Siddiq had been present so his account would fit all the forensic evidence perfectly. He just put Luke in his own shoes. They were safe.'

'And the warning?'

'I think Jay, Janghir, must have been behind it; after all, he employs Siddiq. The other possibility is Zeb. He was in a foul mood that night, he was desperate to get hold of some money, he knew Luke. When it all went wrong and Ahktar was stabbed he decided to set Luke up. And report the supposed argument to the police.'

Pitt seemed to be considering what I'd suggested. He nodded a couple of times.

'The other way of looking at it,' I said, 'is to think about

what would have happened if Zeb and Jay were both innocent. The security guy from the family firm kills their
cousin. How would they react? Not like this, surely.'

'Unless they actually believe Luke Wallace did it.'

'No,' I was clear, 'Zeb has invented evidence, I'm sure.
They got together after it had happened and worked it
out. The Siddiqs picked Luke out of a line-up. They didn't
know him, so how did they identify him? They'd been
briefed.'

'Not easy to describe someone . . .'

'But with a photo . . .' I thought of the postcard picture of the band. They'd had hundreds done – all Ahktar's
family and friends would have had them. Zeb or Jay could
have shown the Siddiqs.

'As for the warning, both Zeb and Jay were involved in
some serious criminal activity, you know. It could be connected to that. Maybe Ahktar stumbled onto something or
was threatening to inform on them.' I told Dermott Pitt all
I'd learnt about the suspected drug trade that the Khans
were mixed up with.

'Zeb seems to be the feckless one. He has a drug habit
himself and he's a gambler. Jay's in charge. I've not met
him yet.'

'I wouldn't advise it at present,' Pitt observed dryly.
'And the accomplice, the man who was with Mr Siddiq?'

'Don't know anything about him.'

He checked his watch and drew our meeting to its conclusion. 'I will do what I can with this today,' he said. 'My
first step will be to make an application for bail. That'll
put the wind up the prosecution, and I am very hopeful
that Luke will be released some time in the next few days.
Whether they discontinue or press for trial is a matter for
the other side. Now,' he rose, obliging me to do the same.
Held out his hand. Smooth and cool.

I was deflated. I should have felt pleased. In all likeli-
hood Luke would soon be out of Golborne. All down to

my efforts but there was no elation. I tried to work out why as I returned to my car in the multi-storey. Had I expected praise perhaps? A 'Well done' or a 'Bloody brilliant!' from somebody? Was it the remaining uncertainty that undermined my sense of satisfaction? There was no definite outcome yet. And the thought that they would still take Luke to court and try him for Ahktar's murder rankled with me. Hadn't he been through enough?

When I got back to Nana 'Tello's, I found Maddie asleep. Proof, if it were needed, of her sorry state. If she'd had a cough or a cold or even sickness I wouldn't have bothered taking her to the doctor, knowing that she'd get well by herself. But earache was another matter.

Our doctor Moira, who is also an old friend, has no appointment system. It leads to long waits but at least you get seen the day you need to, rather than some time the following week. We were sixth in line. Not bad really. Maddie wanted to sit on my knee. I found a dog-eared Beano comic which we looked at together. She was subdued. Half an hour crawled by. I was hot and tired and Maddie was whining about her ear again. My stomach growled and gurgled. It had started eating itself.

'Sal, Maddie, come in. Sit down,' barked Moira. 'What's up?'

I explained and Moira told Maddie she was going to look into her ear with a special torch.

'No,' Maddie began to panic, 'no, Mummy.'

'It's only a light,' I struggled to keep the irritation from my voice.

'You look into your mum's ear,' said Moira to Maddie.

'Can I?' Her face brightened.

'Thanks,' I muttered, and played patient until my daughter was relaxed enough to be examined.

'Yes, there's quite a lot of inflammation. I'll give her a short course of antibiotics, in suspension; give her five ml three times a day after meals. You can carry on with the Calpol today. Should kick in pretty quickly after that. Make sure she finishes the course.'

'Would it clear up if she didn't have them?' I asked, thinking of all I'd read about super bugs and immune systems.

'Probably. Take longer, though and I'd want to see her every couple of days to make sure it was no worse.'

'Mummy, I need the medicine,' Maddie became tearful.

'Yes, you do. We'll take it.' The prospect of trailing back and forth to Moira's all week and having Maddie off school for twice as long helped me make the decision. And she didn't have antibiotics very often, I reassured myself.

Maddie clutched the bag containing her bottle of syrup as we drove back. I accepted that this would be a short working day. I had to call Mrs Deason, tell her to warn Joey. I had better ring Victor Wallace, too. I'd pass on the information on the stalker, now Gary Crowther, to Rebecca Henderson and let Debbie know that things were moving. But after that it would be bliss to curl up with Maddie and try to catch up on some sleep.

There was a white van parked opposite my house. I felt giddy and sick. I drew up into the drive and sat in the car wondering what I should do. Before I could make a decision, I saw Rashid Siddiq get out of the van and make as if to cross the road. I told Maddie to stay put. I got out and locked the car behind me. I intercepted him at the gateway, my prime concern to keep him away from my child.

'What do you want?' I demanded.

Close up he smelt of Imperial Leather and I could see a nick on his chin where he'd cut himself shaving. He was a big man, large-boned, with very broad shoulders.

'You wanted to see me, didn't you?' he said softly.

'Not now I don't.'

'No? You've been to see little Joey. Now he may have told you stories. No truth in them. His head's totally fucked.' The language was more shocking because of his gentle tone. 'Too many drugs. He can't tell night from day. He's a junkie. He sees things. Things that aren't there. Sad bastard. You should forget everything he said.'

And if I don't? I didn't speak. There was plenty I wanted to say but I thought it wise to keep quiet. Silence as a form of self-defence. All I wanted to do was for him to leave.

'Little girl not at school?'

A wave of rage. For a moment my eyes blurred red and I couldn't see him. I forced myself to remain still and silent, refusing to meet his eyes, knowing that I'd see in them the hot glint of the bully underscoring his threat.

'Forget it.' He turned and walked away.

I rushed to the car and got myself and Maddie inside the house, anger searing my belly like burns from an iron. I locked the doors and settled her with some bread and soup, doses of medicine, drink and a video. All the while the impotent fury bucketing around inside me. How dare he, the bastard, how dare he!

CHAPTER TWENTY-SIX

I wouldn't sleep but at least I should eat. I felt nauseous but it would help to have some food. There wasn't much in and for a moment I felt a tantrum of disappointment start. Wasn't it about time Ray did his share of the shopping? Why didn't he notice we were getting low on supplies, why did I always have to tell him? Oh, get on with it, I chided myself. I made fried egg and mushrooms and cut thick slices of bread. I gobbled it up, drank two mugs of tea and had a banana.

Fortified by this mega-snack, I dialled Mrs Deason's number. Let it ring fifteen times. No answer. I rang Detective Sergeant Hatton at Bootle Street, the man I'd talked to previously about the case. I told him that I wanted to report that I was being intimidated by a witness. I had their name and the registration number of their van.

He heard me out and said he would make a note of it.

'Will that be a formal complaint?'

'Not as such. You'd have to come in and make a statement in person.'

I felt exasperated. 'I can't do that today,' I said, 'but I'd like to make it official as soon as I can.'

He assured me he would keep my call on record.

Rebecca Henderson was delighted that I'd got the low down on Debbie's stalker. I gave her all Gary Crowther's details.

'Well done, Sal,' she said. 'It's taken a bit longer than

we hoped but I can move on this straight away now. Send me your bill.'

'I will, and I've the letters here – I'll forward those as well and the photos I've done.'

'Good. I'll be in touch. We're snowed under – should be plenty more work coming your way.'

'Great.' I needed more work. After all, both my cases were over now, bar the paperwork. I was relieved at her promise of more jobs, though I hoped I wouldn't have to deal with too many Debbie Gosforths. I checked the number for the house where Debbie was staying. Her friend answered the phone and I gave my name and asked to speak to Debbie.

'Debbie, I've got some good news. We've got the name and address of the man who has been harassing you. I've passed it on to Rebecca Henderson and she'll be able to get the court to issue an injunction to stop him bothering you.' I didn't get into what might happen if Crowther ignored the injunction and went his own sweet way. It was common for stalkers to persist; there were calls for a change to the law to protect people from vicious and persistent harassment.

'Who is he?' she asked simply.

'He's called Crowther, Gary Crowther. Ring any bells?'

'No.'

'He's living in Ayres Road, off Upper Chorlton Road, d'you know it?'

'Near Alphabet Zoo?'

'That's right. He lives there next door to a charity shop. You ever been there?'

'No.'

Still no lead to what linked Crowther to Debbie or how he'd come to pick on her.

'It's best if you stay with your friend until you hear from Mrs Henderson that Crowther has been served with the papers.'

'Right,' she said. Plenty of monosyllables. Was she numb from her medication or stunned by my news?

I wondered how to end the conversation.

'If you've any questions about the injunction or you need any more information, you can talk to Mrs Henderson, you've got her number.'

'Yes.'

'Goodbye then.'

'Bye.'

Well, we'd never been bosom pals, had we? It'd been a strange case. I'd never known what to make of Debbie Gosforth, though her situation had my every sympathy. And now I was getting my own taste of being hunted.

Maddie was engrossed in her video. I collected dirty clothes from the children's room and added them to the load in the wash basket. I put the lot in the washing machine and switched it on. While I was clearing up the kitchen I tried to think calmly through the situation I was in but fury – mixed with fear – kept bubbling up at Siddiq's bald threat.

What did Rashid want me to do? Clam up on what Joey had told me? It was too late for that, but I deduced that Siddiq didn't know about the tape or my meeting with Pitt. They'd been keeping a watch on me but they wouldn't expect me to be out and about on the job before school. Hah! I felt a little flame of victory at their mistake.

I rang and spoke to Mr Pitt's secretary, told her I'd been threatened and that I'd spoken to the police. I asked her to make sure Mr Pitt was informed, and for him to contact me immediately there was any news about the Luke Wallace case. My standing in her eyes had obviously shifted, due mainly I think to Pitt's reassessment when I'd threatened to cry negligence to Luke. Now we seemed to be on the same side.

Maddie had fallen asleep again, her face waxy and her eyelids translucent. She lay arms flung wide, leg hanging off the sofa. I stopped the tape and went to make myself more tea. I sat in the lounge and watched her while I drank it. I could just hear her breath, regular and shallow. I shook my head to drive away the fears that perched on my shoulders. I wanted to savour this peace. I was continually surprised at how this child enchanted me, and the endless breathtaking love she drew from me. For all our strife, and we certainly had our moments, she had transformed my world and my memories of life before I shared it with her were faded, shot in the half-light.

She stirred as I gazed at her and opened her eyes. 'Mummy?' She frowned, raised herself on her elbows. I knew what was coming from her expression but there was no time to act. She pitched forward over the edge of the sofa and threw up exhaustively all over the carpet.

Buckets and cloths, bicarb and disinfectant. A shower and shampoo for Maddie, clean clothes. I still had to finish my phone calls. Denise came round to say she could collect Tom when she went for Jade. Great. I thanked her and got back to work.

I tried Mrs Deason, but there was still no reply.

I started with Victor Wallace.

'Mr Pitt has all the information now,' I said. 'I met with Joey Deason yesterday. He gave me a clear account of what happened. He was an eye-witness.'

'Go on.'

'Two men attacked Ahktar; they started to rough him up and Joey protested. He pulled his knife and one of the men, who fits the description of Rashid Siddiq, took it from him. Ahktar lashed out, kicked Siddiq in the face. Siddiq promptly retaliated by stabbing Ahktar. Joey was threatened; they broke his fingers as a memento.'

'And Luke?' His voice was thick with emotion.

'Nowhere near. I still don't know how he got to Ahktar, and no one's got a clue why they set upon Ahktar in the first place. It was some sort of warning apparently but Luke wasn't there.'

'Thank God. Oh, thank God.' He sniffed loudly.

'Mr Pitt says he'll make an application for bail and in the course of that he'll reveal the new evidence. But it's not clear whether they'll drop the charges against Luke and discontinue the case, or take it to trial and argue it all out there.'

'But surely they need to go after Siddiq, for God's sake!' he shouted. 'Luke's innocent – this proves it.'

'Yes, I agree. But it's up to the CPS.'

'Yes, sorry,' he apologized for his outburst. 'Thank you,' he managed.

'I'll send you a final report with my invoice. You need to speak to Mr Pitt now about procedures and so on.'

'When will he . . . how soon?'

'I don't know, I got the impression it would be days not weeks.'

'Thank you,' he said huskily, 'for all you've done.' Naw! Now I was starting to fill up.

'Give Luke my best wishes,' I said. 'I hope they do discontinue. They'd be mad to press ahead, they really would.'

We said our goodbyes.

I imagined him looking out at that lovely garden, the boulder by the pond, the phone in his hand, tears on his cheeks. His faith in his son vindicated. The end in sight after all the months of fighting. Though he would still need to be strong for Luke, who, no matter how soon he was released, would need much love and support to get back to the business of living.

I kept checking outside. The van hadn't come back but I felt stretched with tension. Would they leave it now – wait and see if I paid attention to their intimidation?

Tom was dropped off and I made some baked potatoes with a cheese and broccoli sauce. Maddie was still sleeping; I let her be. There was plenty of food left and Sheila was back in time to share it.

191

'Are you sure?'

'There's loads, get a plate.'

Ray was talking about his course to Sheila; the need to upgrade his computer here at home. Tom was enjoying the novelty of being the only child at the tea table, chipping into the conversation. I found it hard to concentrate. My mind kept creeping back to the white transit and Siddiq's quiet voice with its ugly message.

I waited until Tom had gone off to play, to alert the others.

'I was threatened today,' I said baldly as Ray handed coffee round, 'by a witness on the case I'm covering.'

'Sal!' exclaimed Sheila. 'What happened?'

'I was told to forget what I'd heard.' I knew I had to tell them about his allusion to Maddie too, but I dare not say it. It was as though I'd give life to the danger if I spoke the words again. Denial, they call it.

'Where was this?' Ray's face had gone peaky, concerned.

'Here, in the drive.'

'Shit. Tell the police.'

'I have told the police, and the lawyer involved.'

'What are you going to do?' asked Sheila.

'I don't think anything will come of it,' I said, 'but I'd feel safer if we used the chain on the door and checked on visitors. Keep a close eye on the children—'

'The children?' Ray's mouth tightened. He stared at me.

I swallowed. 'He, the man, he mentioned Maddie.'

'Christ!' Ray hit the table. Hardly a useful contribution to the discussion. It made me jump. I knew what he was thinking. My job was too dangerous. I'd brought that danger home, into our lives, into our children's lives.

'It's just words,' I insisted. I wobbled, guilt and fear see-sawing inside.

'Oh, Sal,' Sheila put her hand on my arm.

'Who is this guy?' Ray demanded.

I shook my head. 'You don't want to know. I've reported it to the police.'

'Yeah? And where are they? What are they doing about it?' He was furious, his eyes hard and bright. 'Sweet fuck all.'

'It'll be over soon,' I tried to speak calmly, 'it's more than likely this bloke will be picked up by the police.'

'And in the meantime, we worry ourselves sick about the children, yeah?' He paced round the kitchen, his hands balled into fists. 'Wait here like sitting ducks to see if anyone gets beaten up or—'

'Ray!' I shouted. 'I need your support, not a bloody lecture. Don't you think I haven't been frantic with worry, you stupid . . .' I broke down then, hot tears that made me crosser.

'Perhaps the children could stay somewhere else for a while,' Sheila suggested. 'You said it would soon be over.'

Debbie and her children, packing up, moving out. They'd soon be able to go back home. Had her children known what was going on; had they learned to be fearful or vigilant as a result?

I wiped my eyes with my hands. 'It should be. The lawyer will be meeting the prosecution and trying to get my client out on bail. They'll probably drop the charges too. And they'll decide whether to charge the man who's been intimidating me.'

'Why should the threats stop then?' Ray asked.

'Because either there'll be no case to answer, so what I know is irrelevant, or there'll be a new case and this guy will be behind bars,' I said nothing about what might happen if the case against Luke Wallace continued to trial.

'I really don't think we need to send the kids away. There's no point in blowing it out of proportion.' I avoided looking at Ray. 'I've been warned. Presumably they'll want to see if the warning has worked. What they don't realize is that I've already passed on the information that they want hushed up, and the rug's going to be pulled out from underneath them.' No response from Ray. 'And

I promise if there's anything else, any more approaches, anything, I'll tell you and we'll decide what to do then.'

'I think you should tell us what this man looks like,' said Sheila.

I described Rashid Siddiq and the white van. And I repeated the fact that all this was me taking precautions and that it wouldn't go on for long.

Ray leant against the washer and listened, arms folded tight. When I'd finished he launched himself away from it and clicked his fingers for the dog. 'I need a walk.' Digger wriggled out from behind the easy chair and thumped his tail against it. He circled round Ray who was putting his denim jacket on.

Sheila waited until they'd gone. 'I've never seen him like that. I thought he was going to throw something.'

'Remember that time just after you'd moved in,' I replied, referring to a previous case, 'when I'd been—'

'Your nose, you'd been thumped.'

And drugged and kidnapped. But my nose wore the visible damage. 'He was like that then. He thinks I'm taking unnecessary risks, and maybe the violence freaks him out.'

'He can't protect you,' she said. 'It's your job and you obviously love it, but sometimes you get hurt and he can't do anything about it.'

I looked at her. 'We've never had that sort of relationship. I don't need protecting.'

'Precisely,' she stood up and began to clear the cups, 'and he just has to stand by and watch.'

CHAPTER TWENTY-SEVEN

I washed up. Outside, sunshine streamed in oil-painting rays from beneath clouds dark as bruises. Rain on the way. I gave Maddie another dose of medicine and got her ready for bed. She had some colour in her cheeks and she no longer complained about her ear. Tom was happy to get ready too. I plugged in Maddie's cassette player and put on a tape she'd picked from the library. *Magnus Powermouse* was about a giant baby mouse. It was full of jokes and puns in Latin which I could barely understand and were way above her head, but it still worked as a great story. It was also long enough to last until they fell asleep.

A bath, that was what I needed. It had been a long, pig of a day, the triumphs of completing the stalker case and convincing Pitt to act, soured by the subsequent events. Yes, a bath. Deep, hot, scented. Followed by cocoa, something soothing on the radio, a few pages reading in bed and sleep. Eight hours. I held it out like a carrot on a stick while I dialled Mrs Deason's.

I heard Ray return from his walk, go upstairs.

When she answered, her voice was breathy, almost a whisper. Had I woken her? Was she ill?

'Mrs Deason, it's Sal Kilkenny here. I promised to ring you after I'd seen Joey. I did try earlier but there was no answer.'

She made a noise. Peculiar. It made my neck prickle.

'Mrs Deason. Are you all right?'

'He's dead.'

A punch to my gut. 'What?'

'My grandson. He's dead.'

Oh, God. They'd killed him. I'd led them to Joey and they'd killed him.

'No!' I protested. 'What happened?'

'I had to go to Chester, this morning, to identify him. That's where he was living. He would never tell me, you know, I always had to wait for him to ring me. But now . . . excuse me, I can't talk anymore.' Her voice was flat. I remembered the love for him brimming in her eyes as we'd talked that first time.

'I'm so sorry. Please, Mrs Deason, how did he . . . ? Did the police say?' I had to know. 'Was it an accident?' It was my fault. My face felt cold. Gooseflesh crawled along my limbs.

'An overdose,' she said.

The relief buckled my knees. He hadn't been murdered. One trip too many, that's all. I wasn't to blame. Disgusted then at my selfish response.

'I am sorry,' I said, 'I'm so sorry.'

'Yes,' she said. And hung up.

I shivered. Tried to adjust to a new picture of Joey D, still, silent, dead. I heard the first spatter of rain against the window panes and went and ran my bath.

Cocoa. Milky, rich, just a smidgeon of sugar to take the edge off the bitterness. Always too hot to drink at first. I'd scalded my tongue countless times with my impatience. The phone went. My mobile – in my bag. It was in the corner of the kitchen, underneath Digger. I shook him awake and pushed him out of the way.

'Hello?'

'Miss Kilkenny?' A woman's voice but I didn't recognize it at first.

'Yes.'

'I didn't know what to do. I didn't know if I should ring or—' Debbie Gosforth.

'What's up?'

'It's Ricky,' she cried. 'He's gone. I shouldn't have told him. I never should have told him.'

'What? Gone where?'

'He's gone after him. He said he's gonna kill him,' her rising voice reached shrieking pitch.

Oh, God.

'Debbie,' I said sharply, 'stay there. I'll try and stop him. When did he leave?'

'Just now,' she sobbed.

I tipped half my cocoa down the sink, filled the cup with cold water and gulped it down. Sacrilege.

I scribbled the Ayres Road address on a piece of paper and took it in to Ray, who was in his room, at his computer.

'I've got to go out,' I said.

He looked at me as if I needed my head examining.

'A different case,' I said pointedly. 'This is where I'm going. I may be a while but I'll ring when I've an idea of how long. I'm taking my mobile.'

'What's the big hurry?' he asked coldly.

'Some guy playing vigilante. I've got my personal alarm, too. If he's there I'll call the police. I'll be careful.'

He nodded, turned back to the screen.

'Ray?' What did I need? His benediction?

He looked at me then swung his eyes away. 'I don't have to like it.'

'No. But you could wish me luck.'

A pause. He looked back, his eyes softening. 'Yeah.' A small, rueful smile. 'Good luck.'

Of course I checked for the white van before leaving the house. Nothing. I drove as fast as I could, breaking the speed limit when it looked safe to do so but retaining control of the car. It was twilight. The rain was steady

– a summer downpour that would make mud puddles on parched lawns and bruise the petals of large flowers. The wind had dropped and it was quite warm.

Adrenalin had me completely wired. Everything was clearer, brighter. The vermilion of the street lamps, the patterns of headlights fractured by raindrops on the windscreen. I could smell the faint fruity scent of the sewers as they rose with the deluge.

As soon as I drew near the house in Ayres Road I knew Ricky had beaten me to it. Light spilled from the open front door. I ran from the car into the house. There were thumps and a scream from the room to my left.

'Ricky!' I yelled. 'Ricky!'

I thrust the door open. The atmosphere of violence ran along my nerves, gripped my stomach.

The man was on his knees, his back to me. Above him, staggering and panting hard stood Ricky. He had bloody fists and blood on his T-shirt.

'Ricky, stop it!' I shouted.

He kicked out. There was a crunch, the man yelped and keeled over onto his side. Curled up into a ball. He was crying. I felt bile in my throat and a flame of rage leaping through me.

'Stop it, you stupid prat, stop it,' the anger in my voice was hard as granite. Primal. I had no fear. Ricky swayed, drunk on bloodlust, looked at me. 'You stupid, fucking idiot!' I bawled. 'That's not him. Do you understand? You stupid bastard, that's not even Gary Crowther. It's the wrong man. You've got the wrong man. Are you proud of yourself now?'

He blinked.

There was a noise behind me. It was Jules, the neighbour, without her silver lamé.

'What the fuck's going on?' she demanded. She peered round me to see the carnage. 'Friggin' 'ell.'

'Ring an ambulance and the police,' I instructed her. She blinked at me. 'Now!' I barked.

'All right, keep yer hair on!' she retorted and went out.

Ricky stood there. No idea what to do. I was still shaking with fury. 'Sit down,' I said sharply.

'But Debbie said—'

'Sit down and shut up. You can tell it to the police.'

I knelt beside the man called Chris McPherson. His face was awash with blood, it bubbled from his nose. His eyes were shut, swollen – one of his eyelids was split. He held his hands clasped together against his mouth. He was still trembling and crying softly. I spoke to him quietly, trying to reassure him. 'It's over now. It's all right. The ambulance is coming. You're going to hospital. You're going to be all right.' I put my hand lightly on his shoulder and repeated the words over and over, blanking out everything else. Blanking out the awful thought that I was culpable. If I hadn't told Debbie where Crowther lived, this wouldn't have happened, would it? Not now, not tonight, not like this.

'They're on the way,' said Jules, 'what happened then?'

I was silent.

Within seconds I heard the sound of the siren followed by the pulse of blue light. I moved aside to let the ambulance men past.

They checked Chris, exchanged some words with each other and one of them went back out to the ambulance.

'What happened here then?' asked the other.

A beat or two. No one spoke then I said, 'He was attacked.' I nodded towards Ricky. 'Beaten up. We called the police as well.' I looked at Chris McPherson. 'Will he be all right?'

'I think so. He's got cracked ribs, a broken nose, and his eye's a mess. They'll need to look at that. They'll keep him in, check for concussion, internal damage. He's still conscious, that's a good sign. You a relative?'

'No.'

He looked at Jules; she shook her head. He didn't bother asking Ricky. His mate returned with a stretcher. They lifted Chris onto it and covered him with a cellular blanket. 'Going on his own then?'

'Nah, I'll go with him,' said Jules. 'Can't leave him by himself. There might be people he wants to tell. Poor sod. I'll get me bag. And you,' she paused on her way out, looked at Ricky, 'yer sad bastard, I hope they send you down for a good stretch.'

The police arrived and talked with one of the ambulance men in the hallway. They came into the room.

'Bit of a mess,' commented one of them, referring to Chris.

'Come on, son,' said his mate in a thick scouse accent. 'You come along with us now.'

Ricky still looked dazed. 'But Debbie said he lived here.' As if it would all have been hunky dory if only he'd battered the right guy. 'I thought—'

'No, you didn't,' I said. 'You didn't think at all. You just . . .' I couldn't continue.

They'd all gone. I sat on the bottom stair, my arms wrapped tight around my knees. Trying to warm up inside where my guts were iced with rage and fatigue and fear. The front door was still open and I could hear the noises of the city; a plane climbing steeply, the squeal of a bus braking, the sibilance of cars on wet tarmac. I could see the drizzle floating down beneath the street lamp.

Where was Gary Crowther tonight? Round at Debbie's again, keeping vigil, watching, waiting? Thrilled by his obsession. Mentally composing more fevered letters of spite and sexual hatred to write on his return? Or off on some mundane business, working shifts, visiting family, catching a late-night movie?

I sat and let my mind meander. Recalled the sound of

crying, my own voice screaming at Ricky: *'It's the wrong man!'* Joey D, dead now, Joey with his shades and his knife. Joey watching, yelling: *'Ahktar! Ahktar! He needs an ambulance.'* Siddiq's sidekick shrieking; *'You done wrong, man.'* The wrong man . . . wrong man. Zeb and Ahktar, side by side, by the dance floor, matching jackets. Not wrong man . . . *the* wrong man. And then I knew.

So tired. I ought to leave the house in Ayres Road but the effort of getting up seemed beyond me. In a minute, I promised myself. In a minute.

It took five. Before I left I dialled Ray. Told him I wouldn't be long.

I put my face up to the sky, charcoal grey now, and let the mist fall on my skin. My throat was raw from roaring at Ricky. I moved to the car but he caught me by the arm.

I turned, sudden anger flaring again. I was ready to shake him off. Tell him about the injunction, tell him about Chris McPherson. No longer frightened of the sad man in the old suit and his cruel infatuation.

I turned and Rashid Siddiq said, 'We'll take my car. There's somebody wants to see you.'

201

CHAPTER TWENTY-EIGHT

He kept my arm bent up behind my back to steer me towards a dark car, a Volvo, parked nearby. Of course, they wouldn't just have the white van, they could use that to spook me but they had plenty of cars to choose from. It hadn't even occurred to me; I'd only been looking for the transit. Stupid.

I debated whether to try getting out of his grip. The knowledge that he was in charge of security for Jay, that he had been used to send a little warning when required made me hesitate. I didn't think my limited self-defence moves would be adequate to escape.

When we reached the car he clasped both my wrists together behind me in one of his huge hands and frisked me with the other. He removed my mobile phone, purse and personal alarm and pocketed them.

'Hey,' I started to protest.

Swiftly he grabbed my hair and slammed my face against the car. The wave of pain made me retch.

'Shit.' He moved back a little, freaked at the prospect of vomit on his shoes. My nose began to bleed; I couldn't wipe it. He held onto my wrists and tied them together with what felt like nylon rope.

'Quiet,' he admonished in a whisper. 'In the car.'

He opened the back door and steered me in. He sat beside me. Zeb Khan was at the wheel.

Neither man spoke. We drove north, skirting Hulme

where the infamous crescents had been demolished ready
for rebuilding. Thirty years earlier the slum terraces had
gone to make way for the shiny new walkways in the sky.
Broken concrete, broken dreams. Cracked by poverty.

Siddiq used his own phone to make a call. 'We're on our
way.' Short and sweet.

We followed the diversions through town. Lights were
rigged up to enable the crews to continue to clear the
debris from the bomb and prepare for demolition. The
Marks & Spencer building would go; there were rumours
about the Corn Exchange and the Royal Assurance building. Surveyors were still assessing the structural safety of
the Arndale Centre.

Blood dripped onto my coat. It pooled above my lip and
I licked some of it away I did not allow myself to wonder
where they were taking me or what they would do. I knew
it would unmake me and I needed all my wit and wariness,
every ounce of sense and intuition. Whenever my mind
veered towards the questions, I blocked it.

On Cheetham Hill Road, Zeb took the car round the
back of the J.K. Imports building opposite the petrol station, where I'd once trailed Siddiq. It felt like months ago.

We went into a compound fenced round with chain link.
There were two Portakabins along one edge, illuminated
by harsh security lights.

Siddiq escorted me from the car. Gripping the top of
my arm, he pulled me towards one of the Portakabins. Zeb
passed us, mounted the two wooden steps and knocked on
the door.

'Come in.'

We crowded into the room. The man behind the desk
rose. 'Miss Kilkenny, Jay Khan. Your nose is bleeding.'

'Yes.' I was surprised my voice still worked, 'comes of
having it slammed against a car.'

'I'm sorry,' Jay said. He spoke to Siddiq in what I
guessed was Punjabi, then English. 'Rashid, please, untie

the lady.' He turned back to me. 'I'm afraid Rashid over-reacts. There is no need for this, surely?'

My hands free, I rubbed my wrists where the cord had left deep grooves and then foraged in my pocket for a hanky. There was one in my jeans, back pocket. I pulled it out. Peter Pan, one of Maddie's. No, oh no. I felt a swoon of dizziness. Caught myself.

'I didn't bring you here to hurt you,' he said. His Mancunian accent was tinged with southern vowels as though he'd been spending time in London and acquiring new habits.

'No?' I wiped my nose, it throbbed horribly. 'Why, then? Why did you bring me here?'

Zeb and Rashid had moved back and were leaning against the wall beside the door. Jay gestured at the table opposite his desk. It bore an architect's model of a building.

'Do you like it?' he asked. 'Expansion. We're opening our new warehouse next year. Ski-wear, après-ski, surf and dive. Business is good.'

'Which business is that then?' I said it before I realized how dangerous it could be. 'Looks good!' I tried to cover my tracks.

He paused a moment, just to let me know. 'We'll keep on with the fashion side, the street wear, but this'll open up a whole new market. And we can use both sides to get the ideas going. Kids in the club coming up with wacky new outfits, incorporate it into the leisure wear, turn it round and sell it back to them – après-ski for the club.'

But I wasn't interested in his little lecture on his empire.

'Why am I here?'

He got himself a cigarette from his desk, lit it and inhaled. He blew smoke rings. Very accomplished. My nose hurt; it felt as though it had doubled in size. I'd been hit in the nose before and it hadn't been broken. Would I end up like an ex-boxer this time? You silly sod, I thought, that's the least of your worries. But I didn't let the others come crowding in.

'These rumours you've heard . . . that's all they are –
malicious gossip. I thought we should get that straight.
Now, Rashid here, he thinks there's only one way to get a
result, but I don't. You're an intelligent lady . . .'

Woman, actually.

'. . . no reason why we can't come to an understanding.'

'I don't follow,' I said.

'Joey D is dead.' I wondered how he had heard so
quickly. 'It was only a matter of time. He sold you some
Mickey Mouse version of what went on the night my
cousin was killed. You should forget it.'

Or else? 'I have a client—' I began.

'Who's clutching at straws. He'll get his trial, but I'd be
seriously unhappy if the garbage that junkie dreamt up is
smeared around. Shit sticks,' he said sharply, 'and that's all
it is – a crock of shit.'

No one said anything for a minute then he smiled.
'Besides, it puts Rashid here in a bad light. Most unfair.
With Joey gone it's just hearsay. There'd be compensation
of course. I don't expect something for nothing.'

'You'll pay me to keep quiet?' I kept my voice neutral. They didn't know I'd given the tape to Pitt or that
I'd reported Siddiq to the police. What choice did I have?
If I refused his offer he'd hand me over to Siddiq. 'How
much?'

A knowing smile. 'Enough to make it worth your while.
A bonus. Treat yourself to a holiday – take the kids. A
couple of grand should cover it.' I felt like knocking him
over.

'When would I get the money?' Trying to play it plau-
sibly, cautious but greedy. I wanted them to let me walk
out of there.

'There shouldn't be any problem. Early next week, say?'
I nodded.

'You see?' he turned to Siddiq. 'Negotiation.' He spread
his hands wide to demonstrate. 'Sorted.'

'How do you know she won't take the money and then grass you up anyway?'

'Aw, no,' Jay laughed. 'That would be stupid, very stupid – suicidal, in fact.' His eyes were bright with the threat. 'That's clear, isn't it?'

'Yes.'

'Good. Rashid will take you to your car now. I'll give you a bell. Take care.'

Rashid no longer manhandled me though I sensed his mistrust. I felt my head pulse with pressure at the temples. The knot in my stomach felt as though it was made of hot rock, burning holes in the soft tissue.

'I don't like this,' Siddiq said to Zeb.

Zeb climbed into the driver's seat. 'What about Sonia, the video tape from the club?'

Trust them to remember that – my spur-of-the-moment threat.

'Destroyed,' I said, 'they tape over them after a fortnight.' The bluff worked.

'You told anyone about this notion that Sonia wasn't there?'

I thought my way around it. 'It would help,' I said diplomatically, 'if you could find someone else who remembers seeing her, like you did. It might come up.' I talked as though there would be a trial, that Luke would stand accused. Whatever Jay had promised, I needed to convince the two men who had me captive that the deal was sound.

The silence on our return journey was interrupted by the bleeping of my mobile phone. Ray calling to check why I wasn't back. The phone was still in Siddiq's pocket. He fished it out and handed it to me, indicating I should answer it. I did.

Dermott Pitt's voice ricocheted round the car. 'Sorry to ring so late again but you did ask to be informed as soon as we'd made any progress. Thought I'd give you a try, see if you were still switched on. CPS have been back to me.'

My neck prickled and I moved to cut the connection. Siddiq clocked what was going down immediately. He gripped my wrist and took the phone from me.

'We gave them the tape and the Deason boy's evidence put the fox among the chickens all right,' Pitt's voice went on suavely, 'should be no problem with the bail application and they've as good as said they'll refer the whole thing back to the police. So your Mr Siddiq should be off the streets pretty sharpish. Good news. Thought you'd like to know. I hope to—'

Siddiq cut him off and slammed the phone against the headrest in front of him. 'Shit.'

'Fuckin' 'ell,' swore Zeb. 'I knew she—'

'Park up, off the road,' barked Siddiq.

'Where?'

'Anywhere,' he shouted, 'somewhere quiet.'

My mind went wild with confusion, I fought to concentrate, to make a plan, but I couldn't settle my panic. And I knew that now they would never let me go.

CHAPTER TWENTY-NINE

'Showcase,' said Zeb. He swung into Hyde Road, drove fast past the bus depot, used-car showrooms and derelict buildings. The multi-screen cinema had a large car park. It would be deserted, this time of night.

'She taped him,' said Zeb, 'she taped Joey D. The law have got it now. Shit, man. This is doing my head in.' He swerved into the car park which was large, black and floodlit. The rain had stopped but everything was glistening in its wake. There were cars near to the building, presumably for late screenings, but the far end was empty.

Zeb parked as far from the buildings as possible, at the very perimeter. We could not easily be seen from the busier end of the car park. There was just one car nearby. I assumed it was a breakdown or stolen. Or a courting couple? Hope leapt for a moment until I looked and saw no sign of people, no steamy windows.

Zeb turned round to face us. 'She pretends to do a deal and she's already stitched us up. Bitch.'

'Get out of the car,' Siddiq spat the words at me and got out.

'What you going to do?' asked Zeb, following him. 'Rashid, what you gonna do?'

'Get out of the car!' Siddiq screamed at me. I climbed out, trying to plot an escape route, uncertain where to run. Siddiq gripped my arm again. It hurt badly. 'No one does this to me,' he hissed, 'you're going to have an accident. Fatal.'

Zeb began to speak rapidly. 'Hang on. Think it through, man. You can't . . . they'll know it's you. They're looking for you, soon will be, and they know she dropped us in it. They'll do you for her as well. We've got to think it through. We need to be clever, this time.'

'I'm the one goes down, not you, not your fucking brother. We should have just left it, left Ahktar. If we'd just left it . . .'

'Don't blame me, man. It wasn't my idea to do the whole witness stuff. Don't lay that on me, that was Jay.'

'He blew it. Worried about the Force rooting round, worried it'll get too close for comfort. Wanting it sorted. And this tart pulls it out the bag like a fucking magician.'

'Killing her won't help, will it, eh?' I couldn't believe Zeb was pleading for my life. 'It'll make it worse.'

'I'm not doing it. You are.'

'No way. You're mad, guy.'

'You run her over.'

'Shit!' He shook his head, backing away, 'They'll trace the car, anyway.'

'Torch it, report it missing. Joyriders.' Siddiq took the keys from Zeb and dragged me round to the boot. 'They knocked her down, reversed over her. Freaked out and torched the car.' He opened the boot, got out the spare petrol can.

'And how did she get here? Her car's in friggin' Old Trafford. Use your brain. This is mental. I'm not doing it, I don't want any part of it. You've lost the fucking plot, man.'

'You are part of it, you wanker. You're pushing so much up your nose your brain's melting. If it wasn't for you, none of this would have happened. None of it!' he bawled. His grip on my arm was so hard my fingers were going numb.

'I know that. You think I don't know that? You think I don't think about that? It was my cousin,' Zeb was losing his temper, too, waving his arms as he ranted. 'But you should have known. Hell, Rashid, you work with me and don't give me that crap about the jacket. You need your bloody eyes examining. You cocked it up, Rashid – not me, not Jay, not Mohammed – you! Jay should have dumped you then; I should have dumped you. I couldn't believe it, you killed my cousin and then you tell me it should have been me! Like it's my fault! Bloody 'ell, man.'

He shook his head, still incredulous at it after all this time. 'You're telling me my darling brother's ordered my doing over, 'cos I've overstretched the bank, and you're telling me you've killed my cousin by mistake and you're asking, begging me for help. Threatening to grass us up if I say anything. I still can't believe I did it, but I helped you out, Rashid. Don't you forget that, man. I got Luke.'

'Oh, yeah? You didn't give a fuck for your cousin; you don't have no honour, Rangzeb, none. All you care about is snorting it up your nose and saving your arse.'

'I lied for you. I set Wallace up for you and you, you just pull us all deeper in the shit . . .'

'Shut it,' his rage distorted the words.

'They'll know you done Joey D now. They're soon gonna suss that.'

'It was an overdose,' I blurted out in surprise.

'Oh, yeah? And how come he gets pure smack? Little gift Rashid arranges to come his way once he's tracked him down in Chester.'

Oh no. I felt sudden tears and sniffed them back.

'He wouldn't have taken stuff from any of you. He was petrified,' I protested.

'He didn't know who sent it, someone else made the delivery,' Zeb said scornfully. 'And now you want to do her. It's not my head that's in a mess, Rashid. You're a fuck-ing psycho. I'm out of here.' He wheeled and stalked off.

Rashid lifted me up and threw me into the boot, as if I was a child. He slammed the lid down. It didn't catch. In the gloom I could see the line of light begin to stretch.

I reached out and grabbed it, held it down, my fingertips clinging to a ridge of metal along the edge. It was instinct: a chance to escape. The boot must have looked all right to Rashid. My heart was pounding. I wriggled round trying to get in a good position for climbing out.

I could hear footsteps grating on the tarmac. Grunts and a shout. It sounded as though they were some way from the car.

Cautiously I inched the boot open. It creaked and I flinched, expecting a response, but nothing happened. I clambered out, keeping as low as I could. Knelt on the tarmac and pulled the boot shut. I rolled on the ground at the side of the car and looked underneath the chassis and across the car park.

I could see Rashid beating Zeb. Zeb was still on his feet though his arms cradled his head. Bile rose in my throat; I spat some out. My mouth was sour, my throat parched. I wanted to go and stop the fight. It tore me up to see this, one man staggering as the blows rained on him, the other dazzled by violence and his power to inflict pain. No matter how many times I watched this scene played out, I would never be immune to the anguish it called up in me, the distress and despair. There'd been so much blood, too much blood already.

But I knew I had to think only of survival now. If I headed for the cinema I'd have to cover most of the car park and be visible to Rashid. The alternative was to clamber up the grassy hump, over the low wooden railing at the top and down to the side road. It would probably be deserted. I couldn't rely on flagging a car down to help me, but there might be somewhere to hide.

On hands and knees I scaled the hill. Even at this distance I could hear Rashid's heavy breathing and Zeb coughing. As I reached the railing, Siddiq roared; oh, Christ, he'd spotted me! He began to run my way. Heart thudding, I reached the pavement. Opposite was the Belle

211

Vue Speedway, where they have the greyhound racing. To my left was the Belle Vue Road junction. I began to run that way. I could hear myself gasping, little pleas on my breath. *No, no, please. Please, don't hurt me.* Just like that time before. Did Siddiq have a knife? No, no, he didn't. He'd used Joey's on Ahktar, hadn't he?

Someone would help me, surely. I remembered the case of the schoolgirl assaulted on the train full of passengers. Pleading for help, she was, and they all just sat there.

There was a roaring sound. He was using the car. He couldn't – he'd never get through that barrier. I heard him revving it up. I ran, my nose burning with pain as my feet pounded on the pavement. There was a roar again, a screech and then a splintering sound. I looked back. He'd got the car up the hillock and had torn part way through the railing. A piece of it was caught fast in the front bumper, the other end of it still attached to an upright stake in the ground. One of the headlights was smashed. He gunned the car again and the tearing continued. The wood ripped and split and he was through. He ran it down the slope at my side and spun round to follow me. He accelerated fast. He was going to run me over.

I darted to the other side of the road. I think I had some daft hope that although he was trying to kill me, he wouldn't break the law by driving on the wrong side of the road. Daft, like I say. He simply followed me.

I tried to go faster, waiting in my mind for the impact as he crushed my legs before I buckled and fell under the car. I glanced behind; he was getting close. I thought I could just make it. I launched myself back across the road. I misjudged it and the offside corner of the car clipped my hip, spinning me round and slamming me against the ground. I continued to roll, hit the far kerb and scrambled to my feet. Pain rippled through me and my vision blurred. Go on, I urged myself. Go on! I can't, a weak voice whined somewhere. I can't. It hurts.

My memory dived back to the day I'd had Maddie. Blood then too, and the sensation of being ripped apart, wild with pain. Maddie. I whispered her name. Caught the smell of her child's breath.

Siddiq swung the car back my way again. I couldn't run but I could move. I crossed back, moaning at the pain in my side and down my thigh. I didn't want to die, not like this. I didn't want to die at all, but to be run to ground by a car, killed on the road, breathing my last on greasy wet tarmac . . . No, I wouldn't let him. 'No,' I said it aloud, repeated it in rhythm as I lurched along, 'no, no, no.'

There was a row of bollards along the edge of the pavement, parallel to the concrete walls of the Speedway. In a couple of places there were gaps where big metal gates were installed. I made for the bollards, got myself past them and over the broad pavement to the concrete wall. Suddenly, thankfully, I heard another car coming. I inched forwards and waved my arms wildly. It went sailing past.

I waited. He was coming back, down my side of the road. He couldn't get through the bollards here, but a hundred feet on, by the double gates, he turned the car through the gap and pointed it to face me. He had a clear run at me now, down the wide pathway. I stumbled back onto the road, putting the bollards between us again.

How long could we play cat and mouse? How long could I stay upright? My teeth were clenched to control the pain, my fists balled tight. He roared the length of the pavement, slewing out onto the road near the other gates.

I set off for the gates he'd just passed, dragging my left foot. I used the concrete wall to push against as I shuffled along. He was doing a circuit; it wouldn't take him long. He was going to get me. I was making mewling noises now, little screeches. I reached the gate. Metal bars and wire mesh. A clear view inside the compound to the turnstiles. There were lights on in the main building – a large

213

blue prefab with an arching glass and metal stairwell at the front. If there were lights on . . . I clung to the bars.

A woman appeared, carrying a bin-liner which she stuffed into a skip.

'Help!' My first attempt was too feeble to carry. 'Help, please help me,' I found enough volume to startle her. She was only a few yards away. 'Please.' She hesitated, looked away, then back. She seemed familiar. I swooned slightly. Maybe it was a mirage. I heard the car skid as he drove back onto the pavement. 'Let me in!' I screamed, 'Please.'

She walked hurriedly towards the gate, her face swimming into focus. Blue check nylon overalls, a roll of bin-liners under her arm. She peered at me.

'He's trying to kill me,' I said. 'The car . . .'

'It's you,' she said, bemused. 'What are you doing here? I'm Mrs Grady, remember? Next door to Mr Kearsal's.'

I couldn't handle this. He was coming. 'Please!' I glanced to my side. Siddiq roared towards me. I pushed myself off the metal bars, reeled back to the pavement's edge just in time. I felt the rush of warm air, the stink of petrol fumes as he belted past me.

I looked across at Mrs Grady's shocked face. 'I'm not sure which is the right one,' she cried. She was fumbling with a large bunch of keys.

I watched Siddiq gain the road once more and race down to the other gates. I couldn't get back across the path, I felt so weak.

'Open it!' I yelled at Mrs Grady. The car was nearly on me again.

'It is open,' she snapped, pulling it back. I launched myself through. The car roared past, Siddiq bellowing, the smell of burning rubber. I heard the squeal of brakes.

'Lock it!' I shouted.

'I am! What on earth's going on? Are you all right?'

'Call the police.'

I looked through the wire mesh, hanging onto it to take

the weight from my damaged leg. Siddiq turned out onto the road. He revved the engine till it howled. The air was full of exhaust. I tried to swallow but there was no spit in my mouth and I gagged on the action.

He accelerated fast, drove down the road and did a fish-tail turn, ramming the car towards us, towards the big metal gates. We both moved back. He braked at the last moment. Far too late. The skid sent him careening down the path and into the concrete wall. There was the shriek of metal on stone, the smashing of glass. The crack of the collision.

I lunged back at the gate, face against the mesh, in time to see the car lift into the air and roll onto its side. My heart beat once. Then there was the thump of an explosion and the air was sucked from the night. The fire burst up and into the trees above, deafening in its rage. Thick, tarry smoke plumed. I could feel the heat of the blaze; I was cold. And I wanted, for that frozen, timeless moment, to go and embrace the flames. To lie down in that unimaginable heat and sleep.

Shivers began to tremor through me, making my teeth clatter and my limbs dance. My fingers lost their hold on the wire fence and I slid down to the ground. Slipped away, far away, where nothing could hurt me any more.

EPILOGUE

Shock cushioned me through the next twenty-four hours. And it was weeks before I could resume any normal activity, like walking the kids to school. I had deep bruising to my hip, ribs and thigh, and I'd been running around on a broken ankle.

As for my psyche, I had a few sessions with the counsellor who had helped me after a previous near-murder experience, and I've also been seeing Eleanor since then for hypnotherapy. I'll keep it up until the gremlins leave me alone. I'm getting there. The nightmares have gone, I sleep more easily now and it's been three weeks since I had a panic attack. I'll be OK.

Luke Wallace is home now, his case discontinued. Dermott Pitt has been in touch – he sent flowers. Made me cry. Mind you, the state I was in, crying was a way of life for a while. He tells me Zeb suffered severe concussion from his beating at Rashid's hands, and they still don't know whether there will be any lasting brain damage.

No new charges have been brought against anyone for Ahktar Khan's death. I've asked Pitt to make sure Dr Khan hears the tape or, failing that, someone tells him what Joey D saw. The system might not deliver him justice but he has a right to know the facts. Will Pitt let him in on Jay Khan's role in it all, or not? I don't know. I got a hint from Pitt that the police are currently more interested in gathering information on the Khans' drug smuggling than in their part in

216

the death of Ahktar. Especially with Siddiq dead.

Chris McPherson has been unable to work since his ordeal. His physical injuries have healed, but he has post-traumatic stress disorder. Ricky has been charged with GBH. Gary Crowther has continued to stalk Debbie Gosforth, ignoring the injunctions issued. Until the law is changed he could go on indefinitely. Debbie has plans to leave the area.

Sheila keeps giving me homoeopathic remedies which she swears will help rebalance my system. I've told her it was never balanced in the first place, and as I can't stop drinking coffee they won't work anyway, but she smiles and tells me to take them regardless. She has been helping out with the school run and the shopping and the other chores.

Things are still uncomfortable with Ray. We've tried to talk about it a couple of times but we both overheat too quickly. He is baffled at how I can contemplate continuing in my job after all this, and I am outraged that he thinks I'd even consider giving it up. I have promised to do a self-defence refresher course when I'm up to it. It'll help my confidence, I suppose, though to be honest when faced with a Rashid Siddiq or knives and guns I'd have to be a martial-arts fanatic to be able to escape safely. I will practise running fast as back-up.

They're still rebuilding Manchester; no one knows how long it will take. The Corn Exchange and the Royal Exchange remain closed, along with part of Market Street. The people of the city will be invited to contribute to plans for redesigning the Centre. I think a lake would be nice. Whatever they come up with has got to be an improvement on what was there before.

Rebecca Henderson is doing a job for me now – seeing if I can get some compensation for my injuries. It would help with the cost of the holiday. We made it to Anglesey towards the end of the summer holidays. It rained. We peered into rock pools and drew pictures in the sand. We ate blackberries from the hedgerows and chips in the car. We found lucky pebbles to wish on and wove scraps of bright nylon rope into a mermaid's blanket.

It was magic.

But it wasn't enough.

So I called at the travel agent's yesterday and booked a last-minute flight – a week on the island of Rhodes for my girl and me, leaving Sunday. I used my credit card. I'll miss another week working, she'll miss school. But I reckoned we deserved it, a bit more sunshine in our lives.

You only live once.

Lm
10/13